# Cul-de-Sac Kids

Collection Four

# BOOKS BY BEVERLY LEWIS

## Picture Books

*Annika's Secret Wish*
*In Jesse's Shoes*
*Just Like Mama*
*What Is God Like?*
*What Is Heaven Like?*

## Children's Fiction

### CUL-DE-SAC KIDS°

*Cul-de-Sac Kids Collection One*
*Cul-de-Sac Kids Collection Two*
*Cul-de-Sac Kids Collection Three*
*Cul-de-Sac Kids Collection Four*

## Youth Fiction

### GIRLS ONLY (GO!)*

*Girls Only! Volume One*
*Girls Only! Volume Two*

### SUMMERHILL SECRETS+

*SummerHill Secrets Volume One*
*SummerHill Secrets Volume Two*

### HOLLY'S HEART+

*Holly's Heart Collection One*
*Holly's Heart Collection Two*
*Holly's Heart Collection Three*

*www.beverlylewis.com*

* 4 books in each volume   + 5 books in each volume   ° 6 books in each volume

# Cul-de-Sac Kids
## Collection Four

BOOKS 19–24

# Beverly Lewis

BETHANYHOUSE
a division of Baker Publishing Group
Minneapolis, Minnesota

© 1999, 2000, 2001 by Beverly Lewis

Previously published in six separate volumes:
  *Piggy Party* © 1999
  *The Granny Game* © 1999
  *The Mystery Mutt* © 2000
  *Big Bad Beans* © 2000
  *The Midnight Mystery* © 2001
  *The Upside-Down Day* © 2001

Published by Bethany House Publishers
11400 Hampshire Avenue South
Bloomington, Minnesota 55438
www.bethanyhouse.com

Bethany House Publishers is a division of
Baker Publishing Group, Grand Rapids, Michigan

Printed in the United States of America

ISBN 978-0-7642-3051-6

Library of Congress Control Number: 2017945876

Scripture quotations in *Mystery Mutt* and *Big Bad Beans* are taken from the Holy Bible, New International Version®, NIV®. Copyright © 1973, 1978, 1984, 2011 by Biblica, Inc.™ Used by permission of Zondervan. All rights reserved worldwide. www.zondervan.com The "NIV" and "New International Version" are trademarks registered in the United States Patent and Trademark Office by Biblica, Inc.™

These stories are works of fiction. Names, characters, incidents, and dialogues are products of the author's imagination and are not to be construed as real. Any resemblance to any person, living or dead, is purely coincidental.

Cover design by Eric Walljasper
Cover illustration by Paul Turnbaugh
Story illustrations by Janet Huntington

18  19  20  21  22  23  24        7  6  5  4  3  2  1

# Contents

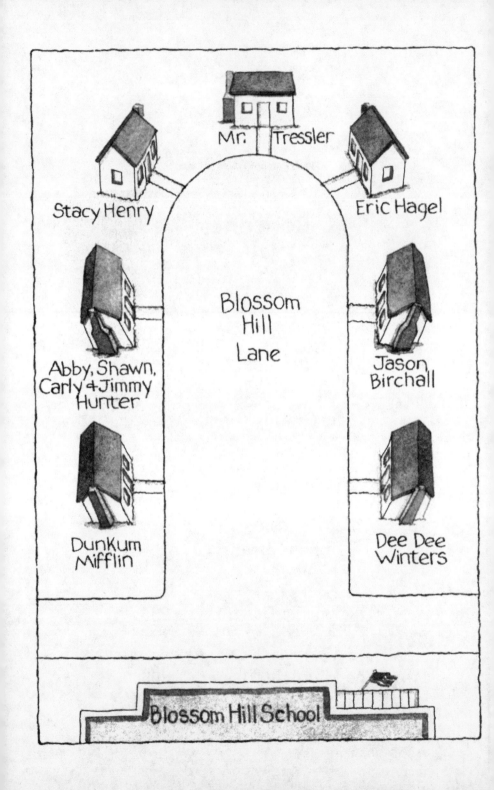

# BOOK 19

# Piggy Party

To
Talon Zachary Erickson,
my new friend in Minnesota.

# One

Carly Hunter watched the school clock. She stared hard.

*Click . . . click . . . click.*

The second hand poked along like a turtle. Three more never-ending minutes till afternoon recess.

Carly could hardly wait.

She turned and looked at the guinea pig cage across the room. The class pet was so cute. And he was looking back at her!

Carly squirmed.

She jiggled.

Her school desk danced, too.

Dee Dee Winters tapped Carly on the shoulder. "You're a wiggle worm today," she whispered.

Dee Dee was Carly's best friend. She sat right behind Carly at school. The perfect spot for a best friend.

Carly said softly, "I have the flitter-flops."

"You're not kidding," said Dee Dee.

Carly was still watching the furry pet. "I can't believe I get to take the guinea pig home. All weekend!"

"His name is Piggy, don't forget," Dee Dee reminded her.

Carly grinned. "Who could forget a name like that?"

Dee Dee smiled and twisted a curl.

"Girls, please get busy," said Miss Hartman. The teacher's voice was kind but firm.

Carly picked up her pencil. She printed her name neatly. She tried to do her workbook pages. But her eyes wanted to wander to Piggy's cage!

"Miss Hartman's watching you," she heard Dee Dee whisper.

Quickly, Carly looked down at her work sheet. She would have to cover up her head. She just couldn't keep her eyes off the guinea pig.

Carly glanced at the clock above the door again.

*Goody!*

The recess bell would be ringing. Right . . . about . . . now.

*Brr-i-i-ing!*

"I call the swings," said one of the girls. She flew past Carly and Dee Dee.

Carly didn't care about swinging. Not today. She had more important things in mind. Things like feeding the guinea pig. Things like changing the water in his dish.

She hurried to Piggy's cage.

Dee Dee came, too. "Where are you going to put Piggy at your house?" asked Dee Dee.

"I might hide him in the secret place, behind my closet," Carly said.

Dee Dee's eyes grew as round as silver dollars. "He might not like it in there. It's too dark."

"But he'll be safe," Carly insisted. "Especially from my little brother."

"Why? What would Jimmy do to Piggy?" Dee Dee asked.

"Nothing, if I keep Piggy hidden." Carly reached down into the cage. She removed

13

the dish of water. She carried the dish to the sink and poured some fresh water.

Dee Dee leaned over the cage. "He's so soft and pretty."

"Looks like butterscotch," said Carly.

"Yummy," said Dee Dee.

Carly poked her friend. "Silly! Guinea pigs aren't candy."

Dee Dee shrugged. "But Piggy *is* the coolest class pet we've had this year."

Carly agreed. They'd had two lizards and even a garter snake before Christmas. But Piggy was the perfect class pet. He was easy to care for. He made the cutest sounds, too. Sometimes it sounded like he was whistling.

Carly liked that. Maybe she and Piggy would have a whistle duet this weekend. Maybe she and the guinea pig would celebrate Groundhog Day together.

Tomorrow!

She wondered if Piggy might see his shadow. After all, guinea pigs were related to groundhogs. Weren't they?

# TWO

Carly and Dee Dee marched home through the snow. Carly pulled her sled with the guinea pig cage tied onto it. "I hope Piggy doesn't catch a cold," she said.

The girls stopped to check on the pet. They lifted the blanket off his cage.

"Aw, look, he's shivering," Carly said. She wished she'd asked her mother to pick her up at school. "We'd better hurry."

"He needs a little sweater," Dee Dee suggested.

Carly laughed. "Whoever heard of a guinea pig wearing a sweater?"

"We should make him one this weekend," Dee Dee said.

"Maybe," Carly said. She was more concerned about getting Piggy inside her warm house.

The girls lived on Blossom Hill Lane, right across from Blossom Hill School. There were seven houses and nine kids on the cul-de-sac. All nine kids were good friends. They even had a club and a favorite motto. Carly's big sister, Abby, was the president of the Cul-de-Sac Kids.

"Are you gonna bring Piggy to the club meeting tonight?" Dee Dee asked.

Carly really didn't want to share Piggy with the other Cul-de-Sac Kids. He was *her* pet for the weekend! "Why should I bring Piggy?" Carly shot back.

"Well, why not?" Dee Dee said. "Pretend it's show-and-tell—like at school."

Carly shook her head. "That's silly."

Dee Dee wrinkled her nose.

Carly pulled the sled faster. She looked at the sky. "I wonder if the sun will shine tomorrow."

"The sun's *always* shining," Dee Dee said.

"We learned that in science, remember? You just can't always see the sun."

"Because of the clouds," Carly said. She knew all that. "I'm not thinking about sunshine right now. I'm thinking about a famous groundhog."

Dee Dee clapped her mittened hands. "Because it's gonna be Groundhog Day."

"Right," said Carly. "What do you think about that groundhog in Pennsylvania? *He's* the one who sees his shadow every year—or not," Carly said.

Dee Dee raised her eyebrows. "It doesn't make sense, does it?"

Carly agreed. "An old groundhog crawls out of his hole and sees his shadow. So what! Is it *really* a sign that we're stuck with six more weeks of winter?"

"It oughta be the other way around," Dee Dee said. "If the sun's shining when the groundhog comes out, that should mean it's the *end* of winter. Right?"

"Yep. The whole thing is mixed up," Carly said.

She thought of the cute guinea pig.

Maybe Piggy would know if their long, snowy winter was almost over. Maybe he'd know something about the secret of the groundhog. And the shadow.

Maybe . . .

# Three

Carly and Dee Dee carried the guinea pig cage inside.

"I have an idea," Carly told Dee Dee.

"What is it?" Dee Dee asked.

"Wait and see," said Carly. They hurried down the hallway to Carly's bedroom.

"Aw, please?" Dee Dee pleaded. "We're best friends, aren't we?" She'd used that line to hear secrets before.

Carly didn't say a word.

"When's the idea gonna happen?" asked Dee Dee.

"Tomorrow at high noon," Carly said. She hoped there was a ring of mystery in her voice.

Dee Dee sat on the edge of Carly's bed. "Is this about Groundhog Day?" she asked.

Carly felt like being a little tricky. "I'm going to find out if spring is coming soon."

Dee Dee's eyes grew wide again. "How?"

"Just show up here tomorrow. Twelve o'clock sharp." Carly went to the window and pulled back the curtains. She searched the sky. Heavy snow clouds hung low.

Dee Dee came over and stood by the window, too. "Carly Hunter, you're up to something. I just know it!"

Carly knew Dee Dee couldn't keep a secret. It was almost impossible!

"You can tell me," Dee Dee said. Her big brown eyes were ready to pop.

"No way," Carly said, laughing. She went to the cage and saw that Piggy had stopped shaking. "Look, he's warming up."

Dee Dee was begging. "C'mon, Carly! Don't change the subject. Tell me what's gonna happen tomorrow!"

"I won't spoil the surprise," Carly said. "It's a Groundhog Day secret." And she made her voice sound extra sneaky.

"Please?" Dee Dee begged.

Carly knelt beside Piggy's cage. She didn't want to be mean, or make Dee Dee mad at her. She wanted to have fun on Groundhog Day. She was tired of all the cold and snow. Carly had to find out if winter was nearly over.

But Dee Dee was still pleading. "I'll do anything you say, if you just tell me."

"Okay, okay," Carly said, finally giving in.

Dee Dee danced around the room. "Hooray!"

"But you *have* to keep it a secret," Carly said.

"I can do that," Dee Dee replied.

Carly really hoped so.

# Four

arly sat beside Dee Dee on the floor.

Time for the Cul-de-Sac Kids club meeting. They usually met at Dunkum's house. He had the biggest basement. And his parents didn't mind.

Dunkum's real name was Edward, but everyone called him Dunkum. He could slam-dunk most any basketball. He was that tall!

The Cul-de-Sac Kids always took off their shoes before a meeting. They lined them up in a row.

Carly stared at the neat row of snow boots. She could hardly wait to wear tennis shoes again. And sandals and shorts. And go swimming with the warm sun shining down. . . .

"The meeting will come to order," Abby said. She was sitting in the giant beanbag. It was the president's chair.

"Where's Piggy?" Dee Dee whispered to Carly.

Carly said, "I left him at home. He's hiding."

Dee Dee had a crooked smile. "Did you hide him in the you-know-what place?"

"Maybe I did, maybe I didn't," Carly said.

Dee Dee twisted her short, wavy hair. "Don't be snooty."

"Listen to the president," Carly replied. "Abby's talking."

Abby was shaking her head. "Excuse me, girls. We're trying to have a meeting here."

Dunkum Mifflin wagged his finger at Carly and Dee Dee. "Nobody talks when the president is talking."

Eric Hagel turned around and stared. His eyes weren't blinking at all.

"It's not nice to stare, Eric," Dee Dee hissed.

Carly poked Dee Dee in the ribs. "Be quiet!"

"I don't feel like it!" Dee Dee hollered.

Jason Birchall made a face at Carly and Dee Dee. "You two better watch it," he said.

Stacy Henry put her hands over her ears.

Shawn and Jimmy frowned at Carly and Dee Dee. Then they chattered to each other in Korean.

Dee Dee stood up. She looked down at Carly. Then she twirled a curl with her finger.

Carly wondered what Dee Dee was up to. She felt jittery.

Dee Dee raised her hand to speak.

"Yes, Dee Dee?" Abby said from the front of the room.

"Carly's hiding a guinea pig in her closet," Dee Dee blurted. "She doesn't want anyone to know."

*How could she do this to me?* Carly wondered.

"It's true, just ask her," Dee Dee was saying.

"It's *not* true!" Carly yelled back. She wasn't lying. She was hiding Piggy *behind* the closet wall.

Abby jumped out of her beanbag chair. "I think we'd better call this meeting quits," she said.

Dee Dee sat right down. "We'll be quiet. We promise."

Abby nodded her head. "It's been a long and cold winter. Everyone's cranky. Maybe we should wait till spring for the next meeting."

Carly got up and headed for her snow boots. "Abby's right. We're fussy, and we can't help it."

Dee Dee crossed her arms and pouted. "Blame it on the weather," she muttered.

"Pout if you want," Carly said. "I'm leaving."

All the kids were staring at her now.

But Carly didn't care. Her stomach did a flip-flop.

Dee Dee was such a blabbermouth!

# Five

Carly slid open the skinny door in the closet wall. She flicked on her flashlight.

The guinea pig darted to the corner of the cage.

"Sorry about that," Carly said. She shined the light away from his cage. She wanted to keep Piggy company. She wanted to talk to someone. Even a guinea pig was better than Dee Dee Winters!

"The club meeting was horrible tonight. Capital H!" she told Piggy.

The guinea pig rattled his cage.

"Goody, you understand." She reached inside to lift him out. "You're lonely, aren't you?"

Piggy made cute little clicking sounds.

"I'm sorry I had to leave you here." She stroked his soft fur coat.

Piggy seemed to enjoy being petted.

"My best friend blabbed to everyone about your hiding place," she said. "I'll have to keep a close watch on you all weekend. I must take good care of you. Miss Hartman said so."

Piggy seemed to listen. He put his tiny face near her neck.

"Do you have a secret?" Carly leaned her ear down. "Do you know when spring is coming?" she asked. "Like that old groundhog in Pennsylvania?"

She thought of all the icky weather they'd had. One blizzard after another. Everybody was sick of it. Carly most of all!

"Will your cousin see his shadow tomorrow?" she whispered.

Piggy began to whistle loudly.

"Is that an answer?" She had to laugh. "Can you whistle a tune?"

He kept up the shrill sound.

"Let's have a duet." She tried her best to make up a song.

Then . . .

*Bam, bam!*

Someone was pounding on the closet door.

She stopped whistling and held her breath. She didn't want to talk to anyone. Especially not bigmouth Dee Dee!

But Piggy kept whistling. Loudly.

"Sh-h!" she whispered to the guinea pig.

But he continued his Piggy tune.

"I know you're in there, Carly," a voice called through the door.

It was Abby.

*Oh no!* thought Carly. *She'll scold me about the meeting!*

Carly leaned hard against the door.

"Listen," Abby said. "You're not in trouble."

"Go away!" Carly shouted. She felt Piggy tremble in her hand.

"I need to talk to you," Abby insisted.

"What about?"

"About your secret," said Abby.

"What secret?" Carly asked.

"Your idea," Abby said. "Your weather experiment."

Carly did a gulp. "Experiment?" she said. But she knew what Abby meant. Someone had let her secret slip. And she knew who that *someone* was.

"Dee Dee told everyone about your plan," Abby said.

*I knew it,* Carly thought.

"Let me in," Abby called. "Please?"

"Are you mad at me?" Carly asked.

"Why should I be?" Abby said.

Carly waited for her sister to say more.

But Abby was quiet.

At last, Carly slid open the door. "I'm sorry about the meeting . . . the way I acted. It wasn't very nice."

Abby smiled. "Don't worry about it," she said. "But tell me about your idea. It sounds *very* exciting. All of us are dying to know if winter is over."

Carly gladly let her big sister into the secret place.

They had their own private club meeting. Just two sisters.

And a butterscotch guinea pig.

# Six

Carly slept with Piggy that night. She didn't put the guinea pig under the covers. But she scooted the cage up close to her bed.

"How's that?" she asked. "You'll be safe here."

The ball of puff looked sleepy. He'd made a little nest of cedar chips in his cage.

"Ready to dream about springtime?" Carly hoped so. "Now we'll say our prayers."

Piggy made three clicking sounds. Soft, sleepy ones.

Carly knelt beside her bed. She began to pray. "Dear Lord, please don't let Piggy see his shadow tomorrow. We want some warm weather as soon as possible. It's okay if the

Pennsylvania groundhog sees *his* shadow, though. Amen."

She turned out the light and climbed into bed.

"Good night, Piggy," she said. "Sweet dreams of spring."

■ ■ ■

In the middle of the night, Carly opened her eyes. She thought she saw a misty shadow.

She strained her eyes to see. But the bedroom was dark.

"Where's my flashlight?" she mumbled to herself.

Then she remembered. She reached down to the floor and found it. She pointed the light at the shadow.

"Oh no!" she gasped.

It was a Jimmy-shaped shadow!

She sat straight up in bed. "What are you doing?"

"I play with Piggy," Jimmy said. The guinea pig was sitting on his shoulder.

"Better be careful with my pet," she demanded.

"Piggy not just yours." Jimmy had a weird

smile. "Piggy belong to all Miss Hartman's class. Jimmy too!"

"But I'm supposed to take care of him." Carly reached for Piggy.

Jimmy backed away. "He like riding here. Piggy like me better than you."

"You're wrong. He'll fall and get hurt," Carly said.

Jimmy began to spin in a circle. Around and around he whirled. He was laughing loudly. He was sure to wake up the whole family!

"Please stop!" Carly said.

But Jimmy kept spinning. And laughing.

Poor Piggy. He was making his dear little whistle sounds. Only now they weren't so little. They were so loud, Carly had to cover her ears.

And she was crying. "Please, Jimmy, please!"

■ ■ ■

When she opened her eyes, Carly saw her mother.

"Oh . . . where am I?" Carly asked.

34

"You're right here in your bed, sweetie," said Mother.

"But Jimmy was twirling Piggy and . . ."

"You were probably dreaming," Mother said. "Jimmy's in his bed sound asleep." She touched Carly's face.

"I thought Piggy might get sick. All that spinning. He could have fallen . . . could have died."

"Honey, look," Mother said, pointing to the cage. "The guinea pig is perfectly safe."

Carly leaned over her bed to see. Piggy was still curled up in his bed of wood chips. "It *was* a dream. But it seemed so real."

Mother was smiling. "Are you ready to go back to sleep?"

"Just a minute." Carly reached into the cage and stroked Piggy's fuzzy head. "Now I'm ready."

Her mother tiptoed to the door. "See you in the morning."

"Okay. And no more bad dreams," Carly said.

She really, *really* hoped not.

# Seven

It was Groundhog Day.

Carly slid Piggy's cage next to her kitchen chair. She sat down for breakfast.

Jimmy slurped his milk across the table. His straight black hair was still damp from his bath. "Why Carly take little pig everywhere?" he asked.

"Because I'm in charge of Piggy," Carly said. "And he isn't a pig."

Jimmy nodded. "I know name of class pet. Miss Hartman tell me, too."

Carly still wanted to protect Piggy. She didn't know what Jimmy might do. Especially after her horrible dream.

Mother brought over a plate of hot waffles.

"It's time for the blessing," she said. "Who would like to pray?"

Abby raised her hand. "I'll say grace."

When the prayer was finished, Mother said, "Dee Dee called earlier."

Carly perked up her ears. "What did she say?"

"She wants to bring Mister Whiskers over for Groundhog Day." Mother was frowning. "Why does she want to bring her cat here?" she asked.

"Because Carly have secret party," Jimmy said, grinning.

Carly ignored her brother's words. "What did you tell Dee Dee?" Carly asked her mother.

Mother smiled. "I told her to call back after breakfast."

Shawn's eyes lit up. "Can all the cul-de-sac pets come for party?" he asked. "We will see if winter is done."

Carly wasn't so sure. Dee Dee had no right to spoil Carly's experiment. It was *her* idea, after all. A private party for just Piggy and her.

"Can Jason bring Croaker?" Jimmy asked,

too. Croaker was the only frog in the cul-de-sac.

Abby poured orange juice into her glass. "It's Carly's party," she said. "She'll decide who comes or not."

Jimmy was whining. "But *I* want to come."

"It's up to Carly to invite you. But only if she wants to."

Carly thought about that. Abby was being kind. She wished Dee Dee wasn't so selfish. It would be lots of fun with all the pets looking for their shadows. That is, *if* the sun was shining.

But Carly hoped the sun wouldn't shine at all. Not today. Then spring would come for sure!

Carly ate her breakfast. But she glanced around the table at her brothers, Shawn and Jimmy. And Abby, too. They looked very eager. Like they couldn't wait for Carly to decide something.

"Mommy make hot cocoa for the party," Jimmy suggested.

Abby's eyes lit up, but she was still.

"We can bake cookies, too," Shawn said. "To go with hot cocoa."

The kids were dying to come to her party. "Okay," she said at last. "Everyone's invited."

"Hooray!" cheered Shawn and Jimmy.

Abby didn't cheer, but she looked happy. Very happy.

Carly felt good all over. "Since we don't have a groundhog, we'll call the experiment a piggy party."

Jimmy spoke in broken English. "We cross fingers for spring. Happy Groundhog Day."

Carly, Abby, and Shawn clapped their hands.

"Yay!" Carly said. "It's piggy party time!"

Abby looked out the window. She groaned. "It's starting to snow again."

Carly was secretly glad. If the sun didn't shine, then Piggy wouldn't see his shadow. Neither would any of the pets.

It was perfect.

Jimmy was shaking his head. "Why Carly make silly weather test?"

"Silly?" Carly pointed at the window. "Look outside. Snow, snow . . . and more snow. Don't you want to know when this rotten weather's going away?"

Jimmy smiled back. "You very smart sister." It sounded like *velly* smart.

"Thank you," Carly said.

Piggy was rattling his cage. Time to feed him his breakfast of pellets.

"I almost forgot about you," Carly said. She sprinkled some guinea pig food into his little dish.

Shawn came around and peeked into the cage. "Tell Piggy to eat very much breakfast," he said to Carly.

"He's hungry, all right," Carly replied.

They watched the guinea pig eat.

"Piggy need lots of energy," Shawn said, "to hide from shadow."

Carly grinned.

She liked the sound of that!

# Eight

Carly and Abby swept the snow off their front porch.

"We're having the piggy party over here," Carly said. "Somebody run and tell Dunkum."

"We are?" Jason Birchall piped up.

Carly looked over at her sister. "Abby's president. She said so."

Abby stopped sweeping. "It's all right, Jason," she called. "Carly already asked."

Jason stuck his nose in the air. "Carly already asked," he repeated in a high-pitched voice.

"Okay for you!" Carly grabbed up a mittenful of snow. She threw the snowball at Jason.

*Ker-plop!* It landed on his shoulder.

Eric and Stacy came running across the street. They joined in the snowy fun. Stacy was wearing her new ski outfit.

By the time Dunkum arrived, a snowball fight was in full swing.

"Stop!" Abby shouted. "It's time for the piggy party."

Carly threw one more snowball. It landed on Jason's hat.

"Hey! Watch it!" he hollered.

"It was a very soft throw," Carly insisted. She felt someone pulling her away from Jason.

It was Abby. "Come on, you two," said the president of the Cul-de-Sac Kids.

Stepping back, Carly lost her balance.

*Ker-plop!* She fell into a snow pile.

Suddenly, she heard a high whistle.

"Hey! That sounds like Piggy's whistle," she said, looking around.

The kids stopped throwing their snowballs. They tilted their heads, listening.

"Wait a minute," Carly said, worried. "Is the guinea pig outside here somewhere?"

Jimmy spun around in a circle. He was singing a Korean folk song. Faster and faster, he spun.

Carly gasped. It was just like her dream. Only Piggy was nowhere to be seen.

She ran to Jimmy. "Where's Piggy?" she asked him.

"Piggy who?" Then Jimmy burst out laughing.

Abby ran to Jimmy. "You *do* know where he is, don't you?"

"Guess who cannot find his shadow!" Jimmy pulled the guinea pig out of his coat pocket.

There was Piggy. He was snug inside one of Jimmy's socks. The cuff was folded over his neck. It made a big, wide collar around Piggy's tiny neck.

"You could have choked him!" Carly said.

Abby shook her head. "What were you thinking?"

"Jimmy help winter go far away," said Jimmy. He started to cry.

"Poor little Piggy." Carly snatched Piggy from Jimmy's hands. "That's no way to help," she said.

She ran into the house. Abby followed her.

# Nine

Carly picked up the telephone. She punched in Dee Dee's phone number.

*Brr-i-i-ing! Brr-i-i-ing!*

"Hello?" Dee Dee answered.

"Hi, it's Carly calling you back," she said. "You can bring Mister Whiskers to the party."

"I can?"

"Yep." Carly explained that all the kids were invited. "And anyone can bring a pet. Except Jason isn't bringing Croaker."

"Because it's too cold?" Dee Dee said.

"He could freeze his toes off," Carly said.

"What about Piggy?" asked Dee Dee.

"He won't be outside long," said Carly.

She was feeling better toward Dee Dee. Lots better.

Carly glanced at the clock. "It's almost twelve o'clock," she said. "We're having cookies and hot cocoa."

"I'll be right over," Dee Dee said and hung up.

"See you," said Carly.

███

It was high noon.

On other days, the sun would be shining.

Today was different. And Carly was glad. She crossed her fingers for spring. Capital S!

Gently, she placed Piggy's cage on the snowy ground. Then she got down on her hands and knees. She looked closely.

"How are you doing, little guy?" she whispered.

The guinea pig stuck part of his head through the cage.

"Do you see any shadows anywhere?" she asked.

Piggy twitched his button nose.

No shadow. Not even a teeny-weeny, Piggy-shaped one.

"Yay! Piggy doesn't see his shadow!" she hollered.

The Cul-de-Sac Kids cheered.

"Let's take a vote on *all* the pets," Abby called.

"Okay," Carly said. "But it's freezing out here."

"We'll make it quick," Abby promised. Snow White gave a little yip. She and Shawn gripped their dog's leash.

"How many pets see their shadows?" Carly asked. She glanced at her best friend. "Start the vote with Dee Dee."

"I vote no. Mister Whiskers can*not* see his shadow," Dee Dee said, cradling her cat. "Too many clouds!"

Eric's hamster was next. "Fran the Ham sees zero shadows," Eric reported. "I vote no, too."

The kids shouted, "Hooray!"

Stacy Henry was next with Sunday Funnies. "My cockapoo can't see *his* shadow, either. I vote no."

"Yay!" the Cul-de-Sac Kids cheered.

It was Dunkum's turn. "Mr. Blinkee votes no," said Dunkum, holding his rabbit tight.

"My turn!" hollered Jimmy. He was leaning over the duck pen near the fence. "Quacker and Jack not see shadows!"

"That's two more no votes," said Abby.

Jason was doing his usual jig. "Hold everything," he said. "I think . . ." He paused. "Yes, I see my shadow! I really do!"

"What?" Carly said.

"No way!" Abby shouted.

Jason pulled out a flashlight and shone the light on his head. "See?"

"Flashlights don't count on Groundhog Day," Abby scolded.

"Abby's right," Dunkum spoke up.

"Besides, Groundhog Day is just for animals," Carly called.

But Jason was grinning. "Somebody has to be different," he said.

Just then, Mister Whiskers got loose.

*Meow! Ph-ht!* The cat flew across the snow toward Snow White.

The dog must have seen him coming. She ran across the yard and over the neighbor's fence.

"Somebody do something!" Abby shouted. "Quick!"

Dee Dee ran after her cat. Jason, Jimmy, and Shawn chased after Snow White.

Quacker and Jack flapped their wings. But they bumped against the duck pen.

Fran the Ham spun round and round in her hamster cage.

Blinkee flicked her long ears. She made strange bunny sounds.

Stacy's cockapoo tried to jump out of her arms.

"This is one crazy piggy party," Carly muttered. She picked up the guinea pig cage and headed for the house.

It was beginning to snow again, even harder than before.

Carly dashed to her bedroom. She took Piggy out of his cage and held him close. "I guess winter isn't over yet," she whispered. "But it's not your fault. Not the sun's, either."

# Ten

The Cul-de-Sac Kids gathered around the kitchen table. Except for Piggy, the pets had already gone home.

"Time for goodies," Carly said.

"Hooray for treats!" said Jason.

Carly set the guinea pig cage on a chair. "Piggy's the guest of honor," she said.

Jason chuckled. "Some guest."

"Piggy's adorable," Carly said.

"But he didn't see his shadow, did he?" Jason said.

"He couldn't help it if the sun wasn't shining," Carly said.

"It's shining; we just can't see it," Dunkum explained.

"Anybody knows that," Dee Dee said.

"Whatever," Carly said with a grin.

"Okay, kids, listen up," Abby said and unfolded the newspaper. "Has anyone seen the weather page today?"

"I hope it's not bad news," Carly said. She reached for a chocolate-chip cookie.

Abby spread the paper out on the table. "We're supposed to have gobs more snow. All week long. The weatherman says so."

Everyone groaned and reached for another cookie.

"Phooey," Carly said. She hated to hear such bad weather news.

Abby folded up the paper. "I guess the seasons have nothing to do with groundhogs and shadows."

Carly nodded. "Or piggy parties."

"Or Cul-de-Sac Kids," said Dunkum.

"God is in control of the seasons," Abby said. "The Bible says so."

Carly couldn't complain. She knew she should have thought of that in the first place!

*Click . . . click . . .*

Carly glanced at the guinea pig. "Let's hear what Piggy has to say."

The kids stopped sipping hot cocoa.

They stopped chewing their warm cookies.

*Click . . . click . . . click . . .*

"Does he *really* talk?" asked Eric.

"What's he trying to say?" asked Stacy.

Carly and Dee Dee giggled.

"Oh no . . . not the giggles," said Jason. He crossed his eyes and covered his ears.

"I think Piggy's trying to tell us he feels left out," Abby said.

Carly stopped giggling. "Hey! Abby's right." And she gave Piggy a snack of pellets.

"He wants to join the Cul-de-Sac Kids club," Eric said.

"He's not a kid," said Jason.

"But he *is* cute," said Stacy.

"He needs a sweater," said Dee Dee.

Carly nodded. "For his trip back to school on Monday."

Jason frowned. "You've got to be kidding. A guinea pig in a sweater?"

Carly couldn't help it. More giggles flew out.

# Eleven

Time for spelling class.

*Click . . . click . . . click . . .* Piggy made his soft, happy sounds.

Carly put her pencil down. She stared at the guinea pig across the schoolroom.

*I'm glad you came home with me,* she thought. *But now you're back at school, safe and sound.*

"Ps-st," said Dee Dee behind her. "Miss Hartman is watching you."

Carly picked up her pencil. She wrote her name at the top of the work sheet. She'd had her fun with the class pet. Now it was time for work.

Miss Hartman would never know about

the piggy party. That was Carly's big secret.
And Jimmy's and Dee Dee's, too. They'd
promised not to tell.

Especially Dee Dee.

■■■

After spelling came math.

Then it was time for show-and-tell.

One of the boys brought a homemade vol-
cano. He'd made it out of clay, baking soda,
and vinegar. The red food coloring made the
bubbling soda look like hot lava.

*Wow!*

Carly thought it was really neat. She was
going to go home and make one, too.

"Who's next for show-and-tell?" asked Miss
Hartman.

Dee Dee's hand shot up.

"Yes, Dee Dee?" said Miss Hartman.

Carly wondered what Dee Dee had for
show-and-tell. She watched her friend go
and stand beside the teacher's desk.

"I don't have anything to show," Dee Dee
began.

Some of the classmates snickered.

"But I have something to *tell*." Dee Dee's eyes were shining.

"What is it?" asked Miss Hartman.

Dee Dee's smile was bigger than ever. "I've learned to keep a secret. That's what I have to tell."

Carly's heart sank. She glanced at the guinea pig. What would Dee Dee say?

"I can keep a secret about a piggy party," Dee Dee continued. "And about cookies and hot cocoa and Groundhog Day, too."

Carly scooted down in her seat. Would Dee Dee tell about the clouds that blocked the sun? Or the guinea pig sweater they'd tried to make?

Quickly, Dee Dee sat down without saying more.

Miss Hartman looked very puzzled. "What's this about a piggy party?" asked the teacher. "It sounds very interesting."

"I can't tell. Because it's a secret," said Dee Dee.

Then the boy in front of Carly raised his hand.

"Yes?" said the teacher.

"I have something to show," he said and stood up.

Carly sighed. *Goody,* she thought. *Capital G!*

The piggy party secret was safe.

For now.

# BOOK 20

# The Granny Game

To
Carol Johnson,

a fun-loving grandma
who enjoys both broccoli
and chocolate cake.

# One

**A**bby Hunter felt like a jitterbug.

Grandma Hunter was coming for the weekend. The pickiest grandma in the West.

Abby dusted and mopped. She checked under the guest room bed. She looked behind the dresser.

Everything had to be spotless and neat.

Abby stepped back for a final look. "Double dabble good," she said.

Her mother came in just then. "Thank you for helping, Abby. What a nice, clean room," she said.

"Will Grandma notice?" Abby asked. She really hoped so.

Mommy nodded. "Only one thing is missing," she said with a smile. "Can you guess?"

Abby looked all around the room. "Flowers! Grandma likes fresh flowers," she said.

"You're right." Mom gave Abby a big hug. "We'll buy some at the florist."

She looked up at her mother. "I'm going to miss you and Daddy while you're gone."

"We'll miss you, too, honey. But Grandma will take good care of you. And your sister and brothers." Mom kissed the top of Abby's head. "The weekend will go fast."

Suddenly, Abby remembered something about Grandma's cooking.

Her stomach churned.

Her taste buds wilted.

Her nose twitched.

Grandma's favorite foods were yucky. She liked to cook things like broccoli, brussels sprouts, and asparagus. The greenest, smelliest vegetables in the world!

Quickly, she told her mother, "Carly and Jimmy will make a fuss about Grandma's cooking. And you know how Shawn likes Korean recipes." She sighed. "What'll we do?"

There was a twinkle in her mother's eye. "Your grandma's very wise."

"Oh," said Abby.

She thought about being *very wise*. Did it mean eating dark green foods? And keeping the house perfectly clean?

Mom was grinning. "Grandma raised your father. Just think what a fine man he turned out to be."

Abby had heard her father's childhood stories. "Grandma and Grandpa had a bunch of children," she said. "Did all of them eat broccoli?"

Mom laughed out loud. "You'll have to ask Grandma about that."

Abby would ask, all right.

First thing tomorrow!

# TWO

I t was Friday morning. School was out for a teacher workday.

Abby brushed her sister's hair. "Hold still. I'll make a ponytail."

"Ouch, you're hurting me!" Carly wailed.

"Sorry. I'll be more careful," Abby promised. She tried to keep her mind on Carly's wavy blond hair. It was so pretty.

She tried *not* to think about the long weekend.

"When's Grandma coming?" asked Carly.

"Right after breakfast," Abby replied.

"She won't make that horrible dish, will she?" Carly asked.

"Which one?" Abby laughed. "They're *all* icky, aren't they?"

Carly pinched her nose. "What if we die from Grandma's cooking?" She was laughing, too.

Abby shushed her. "Don't say it so loud."

"Why? Because Mommy and Daddy might not go on their trip?" Carly's eyes spelled mischief.

"Grandma won't poison us," Abby assured her. "You know that!"

"Maybe . . . maybe not," Carly added, frowning.

"She loves us, you silly sister," Abby insisted.

Carly nodded. "I know. But she cooks terrible stuff."

Abby understood her sister's worry.

What a weekend ahead!

When Carly's ponytail was done, Abby tied on a bow. "Now you're ready for our fancy grandma."

Carly looked in the dresser mirror. "Goody!" She touched her hair and the bow. Then she turned toward Abby. "Why didn't Mommy ask Granny Mae to come?"

Abby smiled. "I think you know why."

Carly wrinkled up her nose. "I do?"

Abby leaned down. She whispered in her sister's ear. "Granny Mae is crazy for sweets. She only has eyes for junk food and goodies."

"*That's* not why!" Carly said. "It can't be!"

"Ask Mom," Abby said. "You'll find out."

Carly shook her head. "*You* ask."

"I don't have to. I know I'm right," Abby said.

Carly tossed her head. Her ponytail brushed against her cheek. "Okay, I'll see for myself." She dashed out of the bedroom.

Abby sat on the bed and sighed.

When would her sister ever believe her?

■ ■ ■

Abby helped Dad carry the suitcases to the door.

Her parents kissed her good-bye.

They kissed and hugged Carly, Shawn, and Jimmy, too.

Dad's face was serious. "Please obey your grandmother." He looked at each of them.

"We will," Abby said. She glanced at Carly. "Won't we?"

Carly was trying to keep from smiling.

Abby could tell by her sister's flat lips that a giggle might burst out any minute!

Jimmy was whispering to Shawn in Korean.

Abby recognized several words.

Jimmy was telling Shawn something about broccoli.

Abby listened more carefully.

*Oh no!* she thought. Shawn was telling Jimmy *not* to eat the broccoli!

Dad caught Abby's eye. He must have heard, too. "Now, boys," he began. "You must eat your vegetables while we're gone."

"We *have* to?" Jimmy whined.

"Grandma will be in charge of you," Dad said.

Jimmy's eyes rolled around. "Green vegetables make boy very sick." He was pointing to himself.

Shawn's face drooped, too.

But the boys weren't going to fool Dad. Probably not Grandma Hunter, either.

"You'll eat whatever your grandmother makes," Mom said. Her words were firm.

Jimmy started to groan.

He held his stomach.

He pretended to be too sick to stand up.

*Ker-plop!* He fell over and slammed onto the floor.

Then . . . Shawn and Carly fell over, too.

Now there were three kids on the floor, faking it.

Abby shook her head. She felt like joining them, but she knew better. Her parents were watching.

"We're counting on you," Mom said. She was giving Abby the Eye.

The Eye was nothing to fool around with. It meant important business.

"No funny stuff," Daddy warned. "We want a good report when we return."

Suddenly, Abby wished she weren't the oldest. Why did the oldest kid have to behave the best? Always!

She guessed she knew why.

It was important to be a good example. For Carly, Shawn, and Jimmy.

"Okay, enough of this," Dad said. He looked at the wiggling threesome on the floor. He snapped his fingers. "C'mon! Up you go!"

Shawn, Carly, and Jimmy were on their

feet again. But they were still holding their stomachs and moaning.

"Don't worry," Abby told her parents. "I'll make sure everyone obeys Grandma." She glanced at her sister and brothers. "*All* weekend!"

"Since when is Abby the boss?" Carly said, making a face.

Mom and Dad set her straight. "Abby's the oldest. She's going to help Grandma," Dad said. "End of story."

Carly made another face. A sour face!

*What a weekend,* thought Abby. *What a wacky weekend!*

# Three

Grandma Hunter arrived in a yellow taxicab.

She stepped out, wearing her pink dress. A single strand of pearls hung around her neck. And there were earrings to match.

"Let me look at you, children."

*Smack!* She planted a kiss on each face.

Jimmy turned around. When no one was looking, he wiped off the kiss.

Abby saw him do it. She frowned hard at him.

Jimmy shot daggers with his eyes.

But Mommy and Daddy didn't notice. They were smiling, almost too pleased. Especially Mom.

Grandma Hunter greeted Mommy and

Daddy. "My grandchildren and I are going to have a splendid time." She glanced at Abby and the others. "Aren't we, children?"

Suddenly, Grandma wanted to hug again, starting with the youngest.

Little Jimmy got squeezed almost to nothing.

Carly and Shawn were next.

And last, Abby.

Grandma's chubby arms pressed in around her. "My, my, you've grown."

Abby was pleased about that. She was glad she was getting taller. The oldest kid should be the tallest kid.

*Double dabble good!*

Stepping back, Grandma smiled sweetly. "I have the most delicious recipe for supper," she announced. "It's a surprise."

Abby shuddered. *Not tonight,* she thought. *Not the very first night.*

Then she caught her mother's eyes. Her parents had asked the kids to obey. They were expected to be polite. They must eat whatever their grandmother cooked.

*Yikes!*

Abby felt like a jitterbug again.

■■■

Abby led Grandma to the guest room. "Here's where you'll sleep," she said.

Silently, Abby waited.

At once, Grandma began to inspect. She ran her fingers over the dresser. And over the top of the mirror. She looked under the bed and behind the nightstand.

Abby was glad that she had cleaned so carefully.

At last, Grandma sat down. Her eyes discovered the flowers. "How very pretty," she said with a sigh.

Abby grinned. "The flowers were Mommy's idea. But *I* cleaned your room."

Grandma was nodding. "Abby, you're an excellent housekeeper."

"Thanks." She stayed in the room. Her grandma might need some help unpacking.

Then Abby noticed a giant shopping bag. It was bursting with strange objects, including something round and silver.

*Gulp!*

The vegetable steamer!

Abby had seen the silver thingamabob

before. It had come with Grandma the *last* time!

She thought of falling on the floor. She thought of holding her stomach. But Abby was the oldest. She *had* to behave. Her parents would be unhappy if she didn't.

Abby didn't dare gag. She didn't dare faint on the floor. But she *did* take a deep breath. She'd have to eat steamed vegetables tonight!

"Grandma?" she said softly. "What's for supper?"

"Just you wait and see," Grandma said. Her eyebrows flew up over her big blue eyes. She seemed terribly excited.

Abby got her hopes up. Maybe tonight's supper wouldn't include broccoli, after all. Maybe . . .

She crossed her fingers. She didn't hope to die, though. That came easily with eating yucky vegetables!

"Did you feed Daddy broccoli when he was little?" Abby asked.

A smile swept over Grandma's face. "Ah, broccoli," she whispered. "Doesn't it have a nice ring to it?"

Abby listened. She didn't hear anything. "What ring?"

Grandma waved her hand. "Oh, never mind that," she said. "It's the taste that counts."

"The taste?" Abby wanted to choke. How could Grandma think such a thing?

Grandma held up the vegetable steamer. "Do you have any idea what this marvelous thing does?" She stared at it, admiring it. Like it was a treasure or something.

Abby tried not to frown . . . or cry. "Did my father eat broccoli when he was little? Did his brothers and sisters?"

"Is the sky blue?" Grandma Hunter replied. She touched the flowers in the vase. "Are these daisies yellow?"

Abby didn't get it. Why was her grandma asking questions right back?

Of course the sky was blue. And the flowers were yellow. Anybody could see that!

Grandma folded her hands in her lap. "Well, Abby?"

All of a sudden, she understood. Grandma was trying to say that her children *did* like broccoli.

"They ate many kinds of vegetables,"

Grandma added. "Back in those days, children weren't so picky."

"So everyone ate broccoli in the olden days?" asked Abby.

Grandma laughed. "My dear girl. I don't think you understood a word I said."

Just then, Abby was wrapped into a big hug.

"I love you anyway," Grandma said with a grin.

After that, Abby decided something. She would try to forget about broccoli.

She would try *very* hard!

# Four

Ee-yew, gross," Jimmy said at supper. He was staring at Grandma's vegetable surprise.

Abby felt jittery. Her little brother had zero manners. None!

The dark green vegetable was smothered in cheese sauce. But the green yuck poked through anyway.

Grandma's big surprise was a broccoli casserole!

Abby didn't know what to do. Should she kick Jimmy under the table? Should she give him the Eye?

She frowned hard at her brother. She hoped he might look her way.

But he didn't.

Jimmy kept it up. "Ugh!" he hollered. "I hate broccoli!"

Shawn's eyes popped wide.

Carly's mouth dropped open.

But Jimmy was just warming up. "Grandma not love little boy from Korea," he wailed. "Not . . . not . . . not!"

Grandma Hunter was on her feet. She hurried over to Jimmy and touched his forehead. "Are you sick, child?" she asked.

"Very sick," he cried. "Jimmy very, very sick boy."

It sounded like *velly, velly* sick boy.

Abby almost burst out laughing.

Carly and Shawn had trouble keeping a straight face, too. Abby had never seen Jimmy carry on like this.

Well . . . she had. Once before.

It was the night of Jimmy's first bath. He had squealed and yelled. She thought he'd never stop. So Abby had gone to look for her old plastic duck. When she found it, she gave it to Jimmy. He stopped crying, just like that.

Now Abby picked up her fork. She tried to ignore her loud-mouthed little brother. It wasn't easy.

He fussed louder and louder.

Shawn shouted something to him in Korean. But that made things even worse.

Jimmy pushed away from the table. He looked terribly white. He was holding his stomach like before Dad and Mom left for the weekend.

Only *this* time he looked sick for real.

Grandma began to fan him with her napkin. "Oh, dear boy," she said. "Let's get you to the washroom."

Jimmy was nodding his head. "Yes, hurry."

Abby couldn't believe it. Jimmy had made himself sick.

After Grandma left with Jimmy, Abby had a funny feeling.

Both Shawn and Carly were looking at her.

"What are you two staring at?" she asked.

"You're the oldest," Carly piped up. "Why didn't you do something?"

"About Jimmy?" asked Abby.

Shawn's eyes were big. "Jimmy not really sick, is he?"

Abby didn't know. "He might be faking. I'm not sure."

Shawn frowned at the broccoli. Then he stuck his finger down his throat.

"Sick," Carly said. "Really disgusting!"

Shawn ran for the washroom, gagging.

Abby shook her head.

"Do something," Carly pleaded.

"Like what?" Abby said.

Carly began to giggle. "Pour some sugar on the broccoli."

"Good thinking," Abby said.

She reached for the sugar bowl.

# Five

Supper took forever.

Abby wondered about Jimmy and Shawn. What was happening? Were they really sick?

She drank her milk and cut her meat. She mixed bites of broccoli with mashed potatoes.

At last, Jimmy and Shawn returned to the table.

Grandma came, too. She looked worn out.

"Ow," Jimmy moaned. He was still groaning a lot.

Grandma sat down and sighed. She sipped her coffee.

Just then, Jimmy sneaked a smile at Shawn.

Now Abby knew Jimmy and Shawn were

faking. But she kept eating her broccoli. So did Carly.

Grandma Hunter reached for the casserole dish. Next, she put a piece of meat and some potatoes on her plate.

Abby wondered if Grandma would notice how sugary the broccoli tasted. "The supper's very good," she said.

"Yes, the broccoli's nice and *sweet*," Carly said.

Jimmy sat up. His eyes were wide. "Sweet? Like candy?"

"Sure, have a taste," Abby said. "You'll see."

Grandma's eyes popped wide. But she was silent.

Jimmy took a small serving. "Only one little bite," he said.

Abby held her breath. Would he like it?

Jimmy tasted the vegetable. He chewed and swallowed. "Mm-m, good," he said, rubbing his tummy. "Grandma put sugar in broccoli."

"Did you say *sugar*?" Shawn said and dished up a big serving.

Jimmy cleaned his plate and asked for more.

But Grandma Hunter didn't say a word. Neither did Abby.

■■■

After supper, Abby helped Grandma clear the table.

Jimmy hurried past them with his hands in his pocket. He headed for the back door. *Why's he acting so strange?* Abby wondered.

She went to the window and looked out. Jimmy was feeding the ducks, Quacker and Jack.

Grandma came and peeked out the window, too. "Everyone seemed to enjoy my broccoli dish," she said. "I'll have to chop some up and put it in the scrambled eggs."

"Tomorrow for breakfast?" Abby asked. She hoped not.

"It's quite delicious," said Grandma. "It's tasty even with *no* sugar added."

Abby's heart sank. Grandma knew what she'd done.

But besides that, Jimmy and Shawn would *never* eat eggs with broccoli. Not in a hundred years!

"What about some pancakes instead?" Abby asked.

Would Grandma take the hint?

"Well, that settles it. I'll make pancakes *and* eggs," Grandma said with a funny grin.

Abby could picture it now. Nobody would eat the eggs. Not one bite. But the pancakes would disappear in a flash.

Maybe Grandma would finally get the hint. Maybe she'd forget about broccoli!

Grandma dried her hands on her apron. She turned away from the window.

Abby kept watching Jimmy. He was outside in the duck pen, feeding the ducks something dark and green.

*Is that what I think it is?* she wondered.

"Excuse me, Grandma," Abby said. "I'll be right back."

She darted out the kitchen door. She ran across the backyard to the duck pen. She stared at the green stuff in Jimmy's hand. "That's gross," Abby said. "What is it?"

Jimmy blinked his eyes fast. "I . . . I feed ducks leftovers." He stared down at the broccoli.

"But I thought you ate it," she said. She gave him the Eye.

Jimmy shook his head. "I not eat *all* of it."

"But you said it was sweet, like candy," Abby insisted. "You tricked us. Especially Grandma."

"Sugar not work with broccoli and cheese." He kept offering the smashed broccoli to the ducks.

"I thought sugar might change the taste," she said. "I promised Daddy we'd obey Grandma *all* weekend. I was trying to help."

Jimmy talked in Korean to the ducks. But it was no use. They weren't interested in leftovers, with or without sugar.

This weekend was going to be the worst ever!

Abby turned to go into the house. Just then . . .

*Ah-oo-gah!* Abby heard a familiar sound. It was Granny Mae's silly car horn.

*What's* she *doing here?* Abby wondered.

Jimmy wiped his hands on his pants. He ran into the house right behind Abby. "This Sunday . . . Grandparents Day!" he hollered.

"Are you sure?" Abby asked.

Jimmy grinned. "That why Granny Mae come. She come for Grandparents Day," he said. "I see holiday on calendar."

"Granny Mae doesn't pay attention to that stuff," Abby said.

"We see about that," said Jimmy.

Abby felt curious. Why *had* Granny Mae come?

# Six

**G**ranny Mae rushed into the house. She was wearing her favorite blue jeans and a bright T-shirt. "Hiya, kids," she announced.

"What are *you* doing here!" Carly squealed with delight.

Grandma Hunter gasped. "Carly, dear, that's not a polite thing to say to Granny Mae."

"Sorry, Granny," Carly said.

But Granny Mae didn't seem to mind. She was carrying a mysterious big bag. "I brought surprises for my grandkiddos," she said.

Shawn also spied the bag of sweets. "Hi, Granny Mae," he said, grinning.

Abby was thrilled to see her, too.

"There's my Abbykins," said Granny Mae, reaching for a hug.

"Grandparents Day is this Sunday. Did you know that?" Abby asked her.

"I had no idea." Granny Mae shook her head. Her earrings dangled. Her bracelet jangled.

"Happy Grandparents Day!" shouted Carly.

"I see it first on calendar," Jimmy said. He wiped his hands on his pants.

"Come here, little pip-squeak," said Granny Mae. She wrapped her long, thin arms around Jimmy.

Jimmy giggled into the hug.

Abby crossed her fingers. She hoped Grandma Hunter wouldn't notice the broccoli stains.

Grandma pushed up her glasses. "How are you, Granny Mae?"

"I'm terrific, now that I'm here," Granny Mae replied.

The two grandmas hugged. But not for long.

"Is everything cool?" Granny Mae asked Grandma Hunter.

Grandma Hunter nodded with a little laugh. "We're getting along fine."

"Well, I thought I'd come over and help out," Granny Mae said. She looked at the kids. "Four kiddos can be a real handful."

"Can you stay all weekend?" asked Carly. "Then we'll have *two* grandmas in charge of us."

Sure as anything, Abby knew what Carly was up to. Maybe Granny Mae could save them from more broccoli.

Grandma Hunter smoothed her apron again and again. She did that when she was upset.

Abby wondered what Grandma Hunter would think of Granny Mae staying.

But Granny Mae didn't think twice. "Sure, I'll stay."

Carly and Shawn hugged Granny Mae.

Abby sneaked Jimmy off to the washroom. She locked the door. "Let's see that yucky pant leg of yours," she said.

Jimmy fussed and whined. "Who cares about broccoli spots!"

Abby ignored his complaining. "We have to get it out."

*Scrub-a-dub-a-dub!*

Abby rubbed and rubbed. She used plenty of soap. She rinsed with hot water. Next, cold water.

Then she started all over again with soap. But she couldn't get the broccoli mark off.

"Look!" Jimmy said. "Sister make spot grow!"

It was true. The rubbing and scrubbing had made the green mark spread.

"You'll just have to change clothes," Abby said. "It's the only way."

Jimmy's tongue stuck out at her. "I not obey sister," he said. "You not make me!"

Abby sat on the edge of the bathtub. "Don't you remember what Dad said? I'm supposed to help Grandma."

Jimmy smirked. "Grandma not need your help. *Granny Mae* help Grandma now." He darted for the door.

"Hey, you can't go out like that," Abby said. "Don't you understand?" She tried to explain. "If Grandma Hunter sees those smudges, she'll know you didn't eat all your broccoli."

"But Jimmy was sick!" he said.

"You faked it. You fooled Grandma . . . *all*

of us. You hid the broccoli in your pocket," she said.

Jimmy nodded his head. "I not know what to do."

"Just *please* change your clothes," she begged. "And wash your dirty hands."

Jimmy looked down at his hands and the ugly green spots on his pants. "Okay. Jimmy obey sister," he said.

*It's about time!* thought Abby.

She dashed down the hall to see Granny Mae.

# Seven

Let's celebrate!" laughed Granny Mae. She and Carly were dancing around.

"We'll eat cake and cookies and candy," said Carly.

Grandma Hunter crossed her arms. "I don't agree with all those sweets," she said. "And we just had supper."

Granny Mae wrinkled her nose. "Well, if the kids just ate, then it's time for dessert."

"Hooray!" cheered Carly.

Abby glanced at Shawn. She felt like a total jitterbug.

Then Shawn joined Carly in a jig with Granny Mae.

"Excuse me!" Grandma Hunter made an attempt to be heard. "I'm quite certain the children are *not* hungry. And too many sweets aren't good."

*Rats!* thought Abby. She wanted to party!

Before Grandma Hunter could say more, Granny Mae opened her bag of candy.

Carly and Shawn peeked inside. "Goody!" said Carly.

"Candy sticks and candy bars," said Shawn. "Yummies for my tummy."

Just then, Jimmy appeared in the hallway. He'd changed jeans and washed his hands. Now he spied the sweets. "I want chocolate!" he shouted.

"No shouting indoors, please," Grandma Hunter warned. She reminded him that he was sick during supper.

"Sorry," Jimmy said. But he hurried over anyway to get his candy from Granny Mae.

Abby took her time choosing a chocolate bar. Carefully, she unwrapped the paper and bit into it. Any other day, it would have tasted great. Today, she was too upset to enjoy it.

"Let's sit at the table," Grandma Hunter suggested.

The kids headed for the kitchen.

"Let's relax in the family room," Granny Mae said.

The kids turned toward the family room.

"No . . . no," said Grandma Hunter. "We don't want to soil the nice furniture."

Abby turned back to the kitchen.

"We'll be careful," Carly said.

"We not make mess," Jimmy said. But his mouth was already dribbling pink goo.

Abby turned back toward the family room.

"I think we'd better play it safe," Grandma Hunter said. She waved for the kids to go into the kitchen.

Granny Mae nodded and followed.

By now, Abby felt dizzy.

This way. That way.

*Which* way?

After all, Dad had said, *"Obey your grandmother."*

The problem was, he didn't say which one!

It was like a game where no one wins.

A granny game. No fun!

# Eight

It was bedtime at the Hunter house.

But Granny Mae said they could stay up longer.

And Grandma Hunter said to get ready for bed.

Carly and Jimmy obeyed Granny Mae and stayed up.

Abby and Shawn obeyed Grandma Hunter and headed for bed.

Who should they obey?

*Eating broccoli is better than this!* thought Abby.

She brushed her teeth and dressed for bed.

Grandma Hunter came to tuck her in. So did Granny Mae.

"Ready to say your prayers?" asked Grandma Hunter.

Abby knelt beside Grandma Hunter. "I'm ready."

"Why don't we *sing* your prayers?" Granny Mae suggested.

Grandma Hunter's head jerked up. "Whoever heard of that?"

"Why not?" Granny Mae said. "We'll join hands and sing in a circle."

Abby didn't know what to do. She could see that Grandma Hunter was unhappy. In fact, Grandma looked terribly tired. Too tired to stand, hold hands, and sing "Now I Lay Me Down to Sleep."

But she surprised Abby and went along with it.

When the prayer was sung, Abby crawled into bed.

"Sleep tight, honey," said Grandma Hunter.

"Don't let the bed bugs bite," said Granny Mae. "If they bite, squeeze 'em tight. Then they won't bite another night."

Grandma Hunter left the room.

But Granny Mae stayed. "Are you sure you're tired, Abbykins?" she asked.

"I'd better go to bed," Abby told her.

"You could sleep in tomorrow. It's Saturday, you know."

"I know," Abby said. "It's just . . ."

"Just what?"

Abby paused. "I wake up real early. Mommy calls me an early bird."

"That's cool," said Granny Mae. "We need early birds to catch worms. Good night, kiddo."

"See you in the morning." Abby snuggled down into bed.

■■■

Abby's dreams were all mixed up.

Granny Mae baked chocolate cake with candy sprinkles for breakfast.

Grandma Hunter cut up celery and carrot sticks for dessert.

"Choose your favorite food," both grandmothers said in the dream.

First, Abby stared at the gooey cake. Then she looked at the raw vegetables. "I like both kinds of food," she said. "Both grandmas, too."

She didn't want to hurt their feelings. What should she decide?

She took a handful of carrots and celery. And she poked them into the chocolate icing on the cake.

"Double dabble good," she said.

But she said it so loud, she woke herself right up!

Abby sat up in bed. She rubbed her eyes.

The moon smiled through the window.

But Abby frowned back.

# Nine

It was Saturday morning.

Abby opened one eye and stared at the ceiling. She listened.

The house was quiet, except for a whirring sound.

Grandma Hunter must be up, cooking. Probably pancakes!

Abby leaped out of bed. She remembered what Granny Mae had said: *"The early bird catches the worm."*

And . . . the early bird gets the first pancake!

She slipped into her bathrobe and hurried to the kitchen.

Shawn had beat her to it. Another early bird was already sitting at the table.

"Good morning, Abby," said Grandma Hunter.

"Good morning," replied Abby. "How'd you sleep?"

Before she could answer, Granny Mae was standing in the doorway. She had a funny grin on her face. "She slept the way everyone does . . . by lying down and blacking out." Then she burst out laughing.

Abby couldn't help it. She laughed, too.

But Grandma Hunter was *not* laughing. She faced the window and smoothed her apron.

*She's upset again,* thought Abby.

Abby sat down at the table, next to Shawn. "What's for breakfast?" she asked.

Shawn whispered, "Dry potato cakes with *no* syrup."

"Anything else?" asked Abby, worried.

"Oatmeal with leftover broccoli." His face scrunched up like a prune.

"You're kidding, right?" Abby said.

Shawn shook his head sadly. "I say the truth."

Just then, Granny Mae went to the fridge. She pulled out a chocolate cake.

Abby gasped. It was the same one from her dream. Or nightmare. She couldn't decide which.

Granny placed the cake right in front of Abby's nose.

Shawn's eyes blinked fast. "Dessert for breakfast?" he said.

"Eat it whenever you wish," Granny Mae said.

Abby couldn't believe her ears. What would her parents say? But . . . wait! Dad had said to *"Obey your grandmother."*

Granny Mae was her grandmother. So maybe it was okay to eat chocolate cake for breakfast!

Grandma Hunter brought over a platter of potato cakes. They were made from mashed potatoes. Last night's leftovers!

*Ick!*

Next, Grandma brought over a huge bowl of oatmeal. Abby could see the teeny-tiny bits of broccoli. There was no hiding them!

It was an easy choice.

Abby had a piece of chocolate cake with her dry pancakes.

Shawn had one dry pancake with his moist cake.

Abby glanced at Shawn, then at Grandma Hunter. "I think we better wake up Carly and Jimmy."

The grandmothers agreed about that. It was a first!

Abby, Shawn, and the grandmothers marched down the hall. "Good morning to you, good morning to you . . ." Granny Mae sang as they went.

"The early bird catches the worm," chanted Abby.

"Better not be any worms in my chocolate cake," replied Granny Mae.

Shawn was laughing hard. "Wake up, Jimmy! Wake up, Carly!" he called.

Carly was too sleepy to wake up. "I stayed up too late," she said and rolled over.

Jimmy said the same thing.

Grandma Hunter shook her head. Her eyebrows rose and stayed high on her forehead.

She wouldn't have allowed Jimmy and Carly to stay up so late.

"I guess I'll have to eat the chocolate cake by myself," Granny Mae announced. She said it loud enough for Carly to hear.

That got them up. Jimmy first, then Carly.

"Are we really having dessert for breakfast?" Carly asked. She rubbed her eyes awake. She must have thought she was dreaming.

Jimmy ran to the kitchen. "Sugar very good for you," he hollered. "Just like a vitamin!"

Grandma Hunter's lips were tight. She offered bananas and orange juice. And the awful oatmeal.

Granny Mae held up the gooey cake.

Carly and Jimmy were grinning. They chose the cake!

Grandma Hunter's face turned red. "Remember to say grace," she said.

*Probably so we won't die,* Abby thought.

"We could sing our prayer," Granny Mae said with a smile.

"Mommy says *not* to sing at the table," Carly piped up.

"Carly's right," Abby said.

"Better *say* prayer," Shawn spoke up.

"And hurry . . . hurry," said Jimmy, staring at the cake.

Abby blessed the food. And thanked God for *both* of her grandmothers.

"Dig in!" Granny Mae said.

"Be neat," said Grandma Hunter.

Abby spread her napkin on her lap. She cut her slice of cake and placed it on top of her dry pancake. But she didn't take any oatmeal with green broccoli dots.

Snow White, their dog, wandered over to the table. She sniffed around Abby's plate.

"Are you hungry?" Abby whispered. She lifted up the bowl of oatmeal.

Snow White took one whiff and backed away.

"The dog doesn't know what's good," said Grandma Hunter.

Abby bit her tongue. She knew better than to say otherwise.

"Ducks not like broccoli, either," Jimmy blurted.

Grandma Hunter's face turned purple.

Her hands shook. "Ducks? Who's feeding my beautiful broccoli to the ducks?" she asked.

Jimmy slumped down in his chair. "Oops," he whispered.

*Yikes!* thought Abby.

# Ten

**B**reakfast was over.

Abby and Shawn helped Grandma Hunter clean the kitchen.

Carly and Jimmy helped Granny Mae make the beds.

Abby could hear Granny Mae whistling in the bedrooms. And there were giggles, too. Lots of them.

Carefully, Abby rinsed the plates. She handed them to Shawn. He put them in the dishwasher.

It was so quiet. No one was whistling in the kitchen. Not Shawn. Not Abby. And not Grandma Hunter.

Abby turned on the radio. It was time for

Saturday morning Dixieland jazz. Squealing clarinets and a romping piano!

She jigged around the table. She waved the dish towel in the air. Shawn joined in, too.

But Grandma Hunter shuffled past them, out of the room.

"Grandma is very upset," Shawn whispered.

Abby nodded. "I know."

"At least we're safe from broccoli." Shawn laughed.

"Maybe," replied Abby.

But broccoli didn't matter right now.

■ ■ ■

Abby went looking for Granny Mae. She found her downstairs in the family room. "I think we have a problem," Abby told her. "It's about Grandma Hunter."

Granny Mae's eyes popped wide. "What's wrong?"

Abby tried to explain. "Grandma Hunter likes things . . . uh, just so." She paused.

Granny chuckled. "That's nothing new. Everyone knows Grandma Hunter's fussy that way."

"But she's *unhappy*," Abby insisted. "I think we hurt her feelings."

"Oh dear," Granny Mae said. "I was afraid of that. I suppose I should have stayed home."

"No, Granny, we're glad you came. After all, it's Grandparents Day tomorrow," Abby said. "But how can we make Grandma cheerful again?"

Granny Mae scratched her head. "Let's see . . ." She thought and thought.

Then she jumped up off the sofa. "You just leave that to me, Abbykins." And she marched down the hall and knocked on the guest room door.

Abby gulped. *What have I done?*

■■■

Two grandmas were locked away in the guest room.

Abby watched the kitchen clock.

The minutes ticked by.

She and Carly, Jimmy, and Shawn sat around the table. They were silent as they looked back and forth at one another.

"What if Granny Mae goes home?" Carly worried aloud.

116

Abby shrugged. "She's up to something. I know that much."

Jimmy rolled his eyes. "I like fun Granny. She very cool."

Shawn poked his brother. "And I like other Grandma. She give great hugs."

Abby heard several footsteps. "Sh-h! Someone's coming!"

The kids sat up straight . . . waiting.

Then Granny Mae and Grandma Hunter strolled into the kitchen. Their arms were linked together!

Abby's mouth dropped open. *What's going on?* she wondered.

"Everything's cool, kiddos," Granny Mae announced. "Grandma Hunter and I have come to an agreement."

Grandma Hunter's eyes were shining. "You dear children," she said. "You've been all mixed up this weekend. One strict grandma and one happy-go-lucky granny—both of us trying to take good care of you."

Granny Mae agreed. "You kiddos have been trying to please both of us. That's too much to ask."

Abby listened. *What's the agreement?* she wondered.

Grandma Hunter continued. "There's a time for dessert . . ."

"And there's a time for broccoli," added Granny Mae.

"Both are important," the grandmas said together.

"There's a time to party," said Grandma Hunter.

"And there's a time to work," Granny Mae said. "And something else. We've agreed to be a team . . . Grandma and I."

"And," said Grandma Hunter, "we've agreed to a party!" She was grinning.

The Hunter kids cheered. "Hooray!"

"When's the party?" Carly asked.

"Tomorrow, right after church," said Granny Mae.

"For Grandparents Day?" Jimmy asked, wide-eyed.

"Double dabble good idea!" shouted Abby.

Grandma Hunter sat at the table. "Let's plan a big dinner party," she said. "What would you like to eat?"

*Anything but broccoli,* thought Abby. But

she was polite. "We all like pasta," she suggested.

Grandma's eyes sparkled. "We'll have a spaghetti feast."

"With meat sauce?" Carly asked.

"Oh, certainly," said Grandma Hunter.

"Just *plain* meat sauce?" Abby asked. She had to make sure no vegetables would be floating around.

Granny Mae spoke up. "We'll have vegetables on the side. But no broccoli tomorrow."

"And we'll have plenty of desserts after dinner," Grandma added.

"Can we invite Grandpa Hunter?" asked Carly.

"Of course," Grandma said. She looked at Granny Mae. "And while you're at it, invite your friends, too."

Abby gasped.

Was this for real?

"We want to meet the Cul-de-Sac Kids," Grandma Hunter said. "Don't we, Granny?"

"*All* of them?" asked Abby.

Granny Mae stuck up both her thumbs. "You got it, girl. We'll have a pasta picnic in the backyard."

"Invite their grandparents, too," Grandma Hunter said.

Abby couldn't stop laughing. Her jitters were gone.

The Granny Game was the best. Nobody had to win, after all.

Double dabble terrific!

# BOOK 21

# Mystery Mutt

To
Wesley Harris,
who sends me wonderful
letters and likes
reading this series.

# One

It was three days before New Year's Eve. Things were popping on Blossom Hill Lane.

Stacy Henry was buzzing with an idea. Her cool idea had started out teeny-weeny. But during the last Cul-de-Sac Kids club meeting, it grew.

And grew!

She couldn't keep it to herself any longer.

"Let's do something really fun to celebrate the new year," she suggested.

"Yay!" the girls shouted.

Jason Birchall spoke up. "Like what?"

Stacy twirled her hair. "It's that time of year, isn't it?"

"What are you talking about?" asked Jason, pushing up his glasses. "*What* time of year?"

"I'll give you three guesses, but only three." She squeezed in next to Abby Hunter in the president's seat—a beanbag chair.

Abby was the president of the Cul-de-Sac Kids club. A neighborhood club with nine members who lived on Blossom Hill Lane. A cul-de-sac shaped like a U.

Abby grinned. "I like guessing games. Who wants to guess first?"

"I will!" Dee Dee Winters stood up. She pulled up her knee socks. Then she put her finger on her lip. "My guess is it's time to go group sledding. *That's* really fun!"

Stacy nodded her head. "You're right, going sledding together is lots of fun. But that's not what I was thinking."

"Who's next?" asked Abby. "This is the second guess, remember."

Dunkum Mifflin raised his hand. "It's time to think about the new year? Maybe write down some goals or something. That's my guess," he said.

Stacy looked at Abby and whispered, "He's almost got it."

Abby grinned at Dunkum. "Stacy says you're real close. Want to guess again?"

Dunkum, whose real name was Edward, shook his head no. The kids had nicknamed him Dunkum because he was tall. So tall he could dunk a basketball almost every time.

"OK," said Stacy. "Since Dunkum nearly guessed it, I'll tell my idea."

The kids leaned forward. Their eyes were as big as bowls.

"I want to make some changes in myself," Stacy said. "Like grown-ups do every year."

"Oh no. Not grown-up stuff!" Jason complained. He rolled his eyes and stuck out his tongue. "That's so dumb."

Eric Hagel frowned at Jason. "Don't say 'dumb.' It's not cool. Besides, Stacy's idea might be more fun than you think."

Carly—Abby's little sister—grabbed Dee Dee's hand. They were best friends. "I don't care what Jason says. I want to make some changes for the new year, too. Just like Stacy."

"What kind of changes?" Jason grumbled.

Stacy said, "Things like asking God to help make me kind and loving. Good changes like that."

Jason clutched his throat when she said "loving."

*Yikes!* Stacy worried that a full-blown fit was coming.

Quickly, Abby called the meeting to order again. "I like Stacy's idea, too. Keep talking," she told Stacy.

"Can we name the Fruit of the Spirit?" asked Stacy.

Lots of hands went up.

All but Jason's.

Stacy was pretty sure he could say them, too. Jason was just being a pest. But that was normal for him.

"How many Fruit of the Spirit are there?" Stacy asked.

"That's easy. Nine!" Dunkum said.

"I almost say that," Shawn Hunter said in broken English.

Shawn was Abby's adopted brother from Korea. Their little brother, Jimmy, also from Korea, was nodding, too.

"We know lots of fruit from Bible," Jimmy piped up. "American mother teach us."

Abby's eyes were shining. "Shawn and

Jimmy are right. And I think we *all* know the Fruit of the Spirit."

"Can we say them?" Stacy asked, searching for some chalk. "Or maybe we can write them on the chalkboard."

"Good thinking!" replied Abby.

"When we're finished, we'll pick some fruit," Stacy said, smiling. "Each of us can choose a different fruit for the year."

"But we won't eat it," Carly joked.

Dunkum was laughing. "Not unless you want a mouthful of joy or peace."

Dee Dee smirked at Jason. "I think one of us needs the *full-meal deal!*"

Some of the kids snickered.

But Stacy was quiet. She held the board while Abby wrote the nine Fruit of the Spirit.

One at a time, the Cul-de-Sac Kids called them out:

| | |
|---|---|
| Love | Goodness |
| Joy | Faithfulness |
| Peace | Gentleness |
| Patience | Self-control |
| Kindness | |

# Two

"I want more patience!" hollered Dee Dee Winters. "And I want it now!"

Stacy chuckled about Dee Dee's choice. It was perfect.

"I pick self-control," Jimmy decided.

Shawn nodded but didn't laugh. "Little brother pick very good fruit," he said. "I pick love—just like Stacy."

Stacy felt her face grow warm. Shawn was looking at her. "Who's next?" she asked.

Carly's hand flew up. "Patience sounds good for me, too." She looked at Dee Dee. "I want to match my best friend," she said.

"Joy sounds like a good one," Eric said, his eyes twinkling.

"I think you already have *that* fruit," Stacy said.

The kids agreed.

"Pick something you know you need. Something to improve on," Dunkum suggested.

Eric thought and thought. "OK, I've got it. I'll pick peace. I sure could use some of that." He explained that his grandpa—who lived at his house—was going deaf. "Peace is a good fruit for me to have this year."

Stacy thought Eric's choice was real cool.

Dunkum raised his hand. "I'll pick faithfulness," he said. "Sounds like a good one for me."

Abby spoke up next. "I'll take joy," she said. "And afterward, I want to give it away."

"You can't keep joy to yourself," Stacy said.

The other kids seemed to know exactly what she meant.

"That leaves you, Jason," Stacy said. "There's still some fruit to be picked."

"No." Jason shook his head. "I'm not gonna do the fruit thing," he said. "It's silly."

Stacy looked at Abby and shrugged her shoulders. The rest of the Cul-de-Sac Kids were quiet.

"OK, that's my idea," Stacy said. "I'm finished."

She turned the meeting back to their president.

But she felt strange toward Jason. Why didn't he want to stick with his friends? Was there a problem?

# Three

W hat's for supper?" Stacy asked her mother.

"Spaghetti and meatballs," Mom said. She pulled out the drawer nearest the table. Knives, forks, and spoons lay neatly inside.

"May I help?" Stacy asked.

Mom smiled. "Would you like to set the table?"

"OK!" Stacy always liked helping her mom. She wished she could help even more. Since her dad left, it was just her and her mom— the two of them. Stacy's mother worked long hours away from home and was often tired in the evening.

"I'll clean up the kitchen for you," Stacy offered. "After we eat."

"That's nice of you." Mom went to check the noodles.

"Is everything under control?" Stacy asked. She watched her mother stir the long, skinny noodles.

"They're getting soft. We'll eat soon."

"I love pasta!" Stacy exclaimed.

She meant it, too. Pasta was the best food in the world!

Mom turned to look at her. "That's why I made it. Just for you."

Stacy studied her mom. "You're always so sweet," she said. "Full of the Fruit of the Spirit."

"Well, I don't know about that, honey," Mom said. "Nobody's perfect."

"I think you're pretty close," she whispered.

Mom reached over and gave her a big hug. "What's this about the Fruit of the Spirit?" Mom asked.

"It's something the Cul-de-Sac Kids are doing."

"Really?" Mom seemed pleased.

Stacy felt proud. "It was my idea."

"Tell me more," Mom said.

"You know about making resolutions,

right?" she asked. "Especially around the new year?"

Mom nodded. "Lots of people do this time of year. But not everyone sticks to goals. That's the hard part."

"All my friends have picked a fruit," Stacy explained. "Straight from the Bible."

"And what sort of fruit might that be?" Mom was grinning. She already knew; Stacy was sure of it.

"Things like goodness and love . . . peace and joy." She washed her hands and set the table for two. "I'm picking love," she said.

"What a wonderful choice," Mom said.

"I'm going to try to love everyone I know. With God's help." She headed for the living room. She wanted to check on her little dog, Sunday Funnies.

She found him curled up near the comics page of the newspaper. "What's with you and the funnies?" she asked. "I always know where to find you, don't I?"

Sunday Funnies barked playfully.

Stacy picked him up. Gently, she carried him into the kitchen. "Time for your supper," she said.

Sunday Funnies made excited sounds.

"Have patience," she told him.

"One of the Fruit of the Spirit," Mom added.

"That's right!" Stacy said. "So . . . some patience, please."

She poured dog food into his dish. Then Stacy stepped aside. "Now have some joy, too," she said.

Mom was laughing.

Sunday Funnies was chowing down.

Stacy was eager for spaghetti!

# Four

**G**ood morning, sleepyhead," said Mom. She shook Stacy's shoulder very lightly. "Are you going to sleep all day?"

Stacy stretched and yawned. "It's Christmas break, and I'm still tired."

"OK," Mom said. "I'll let Sunday Funnies out for you."

"Are you leaving for work already?" Stacy asked.

Mom looked at the clock on Stacy's desk. "I'll go in ten minutes," she said.

Stacy sat up. "I guess I slept too late."

"That's all right, honey. You'll be getting up early again next week when school starts," Mom said with a tender smile.

Stacy swung her legs over the side. "I'm awake now. So I might as well get up."

Mom sat quietly, still smiling.

Stacy yawned again. "I think I'll go visit Jason today."

"How's he doing?" Mom asked.

"Want to know the truth? He's a pain," Stacy complained.

Mom frowned. "Time to spread some love around. It sounds like Jason Birchall could use a good dose," she remarked.

Usually, Stacy would be thinking, *Icksville!* About showing love to Jason, that is.

Jason was one weird kid. He wasn't easy to love.

Most kids *liked* Jason, though. He was full of fun. Mischief, too.

Even Pinktoes, Jason's pet spider, liked him. So did Croaker, his bullfrog. Jason wanted to add even more pets to his "zoo."

But love? That was a difficult subject.

Stacy sighed. She understood her mother. Love was the first Fruit of the Spirit. And loving Jason could be tricky at times. But she could do it. God would help her!

"You're right, Mom," she agreed. "I'll go easy on Jason."

"That's my girl," Mom said.

■■■

Stacy found Jason outside, sweeping snow off his steps.

"Hey, Jason!" she called to him.

He looked up. But when he saw her, he looked back down.

"Are you busy?" she asked, hurrying across the street.

"What's it look like?" he said. He kept sweeping even though the cement was peeking through.

"I thought we could talk," she said.

"So talk." He glanced over his shoulder at her.

She wondered if she should turn around and go home. Should she even try to show love to Jason?

"Maybe now isn't such a good time," she muttered.

"Maybe not." He kept facing away from her.

"OK. I'll see you later." She headed back across the street. She really thought he

might call to her. Tell her to stop walking away and come back.

But he didn't say one word.

Stacy turned to look at Jason from her porch step. She stared at him.

He was still sweeping with his back to her. Jason was doing what he did best. *Being a pain*, she thought.

"It's too bad," she whispered to herself. "Jason's gonna spoil everything for New Year's."

She opened the front door to her house. With a huff, she went inside.

# Five

After a while, Stacy headed next door to visit her best friend.

"How are we going to get Jason to pick a fruit?" she asked Abby.

Abby shook her head. "Your guess is as good as mine."

They sat on Abby's bed and lined up the stuffed animals.

"Maybe if we give him some space," said Stacy. "That might help."

Abby's face lit up. "If we give him *enough* space, he might feel left out."

Stacy wasn't sure about that. "I don't know. That might not be the best way to show love," she said.

"Sometimes loving someone means giving

him breathing room." Abby blinked her eyes. "Know what I mean?"

Stacy thought about that. "Maybe."

"So we'll pray," Abby said. "And we'll be patient and gentle with him. Two more fruits."

There was a calendar hanging on Abby's bulletin board.

Stacy counted the days till New Year's Eve. "Phooey," she whispered.

"What's wrong?" asked Abby.

Stacy sat back down on the bed. "We don't have much time."

Abby was nodding her head. "You're right. So we better start praying," she said.

"And we should have another club meeting," Stacy suggested.

"Good idea!" Abby seemed excited about getting together again. "I'll call Dee Dee and Dunkum. You can tell Eric and Jason. OK?"

Stacy paused. "I . . . I don't know about calling Jason. He might not want to talk to me."

"Why not?"

She told Abby how Jason had treated her this morning. "He could hardly wait for me to leave."

"Are you double dabble sure?" Abby's eyes were big and round.

"I think he's upset about the fruit idea." Stacy hoped she wasn't spreading trouble by talking this way. She wanted to spread God's love around.

"I don't know why he'd be upset," Abby said. "Unless . . ."

"Unless what?" Stacy asked. She was eager to know.

Abby leaned back against her pillow. "Sometimes Jason likes to be different just to be different. No other reason."

"You're right," Stacy replied. "He gets more attention that way."

"So we have to *help* him think differently," Abby said.

"That's the hard part," Stacy said.

"He's one stubborn kid," Abby added.

"I guess we *all* are . . . sometimes," Stacy agreed.

They listened to music in Abby's room for a few minutes.

Soon, Carly knocked on the door.

"Come in," Abby called.

Carly came in, looking surprised. "Don't

you want to hear the secret password?" she asked.

Abby looked at Stacy. Her face was red. "I . . . I don't know."

"Well, you usually make me say it," said Carly. She shot a look at Stacy. "So . . . what are you two doing?"

Stacy almost said *"None of your beeswax."* But today, she was kind. "Just talking," she said.

Abby looked shocked.

"Want to join us?" Stacy asked Carly.

"Goody!" The little girl jumped up and sat on the bed. "So . . . what are we talking about?" she asked.

Abby smiled. Stacy was almost positive she was going to be kind to her little sister.

"We're just talking about Jason and the Fruit of the Spirit. We're going to pray about that," explained Abby.

Carly's eyes were shining. "I'll help you."

"Good," Stacy said. "The more, the merrier."

Carly frowned. "What's that mean?"

Abby told her. "The more people praying, the better."

"About what?" Carly was full of questions, as usual.

Abby's face drooped. She seemed a little angry. But she didn't spout off anything nasty.

Stacy spoke up. "Jason doesn't want to pick a fruit."

"Oh yeah. I know all about that." Carly grinned. "But I think he'll change his mind."

"That's why we're going to pray," said Stacy.

"Starting now?" Carly asked.

"Sure," said Stacy.

"Yay!" said Carly.

Stacy and Abby took turns praying out loud. Carly added two sentences and the amen at the end.

"We'll be very kind to Jason," Stacy said. "We promise, right?"

"It's almost New Year's," Carly reminded them.

"That's OK. Jason will pick a fruit," Stacy said. "You'll see."

# Six

Stacy's new yo-yo had a rainbow of colors on one side. There was a happy face on the opposite side. The gift had been in her Christmas stocking. It was one of her favorite new toys.

Later that afternoon, she played with the yo-yo. And with her dog.

"Jason Birchall oughta be bored with his fits," she said.

Sunday Funnies cocked his head like he was really listening.

"But you know what?" Stacy continued. "I think something's gonna happen. And real soon."

Sunday Funnies barked and wagged his tail.

"Don't you understand?" she asked. "I mean something wonderful is going to happen to Jason. I just have a feeling."

She looked out the living room window. The street was dusted with clean, fresh snow. Like a frosted cul-de-sac—all fleecy white.

"The world looks white and fluffy, just like you," she whispered. She picked her cockapoo up and held him close.

"Mm-m, you smell good!" She buried her face in his soft, curly coat. "Did Mom give you a bath yesterday afternoon?"

Sunday Funnies didn't bark yes. But he did bark something. She wasn't exactly sure what he was trying to tell her. Maybe he wanted to go outside.

Yes, that's probably what he wanted.

Stacy waited for her dog to go out. She thought of yesterday's club meeting. Mom must have given Sunday Funnies a bath during the meeting.

She decided to take better care of her dog. After all, he was *her* responsibility. In fact, she decided to help around the house more. A lot more!

Soon, Sunday Funnies was whining at the door.

She let him inside. "Want to help me clean house?" she asked.

But he followed the scent of the newspaper. He sat down on the living room floor, right next to the paper.

"Now, that's a good way to help," she said. "If you stay out of my way, I'll get the cleaning done much faster."

She went to the hall closet and lugged out the vacuum. Then she found the plug and turned it on.

*Mom will be surprised,* she thought.

She could hardly wait to see her mother's face!

■ ■ ■

Minutes later, the doorbell rang.

Stacy didn't really *hear* the bell. But she knew someone was there just the same.

Sunday Funnies had run to the door and was howling now.

Quickly, she switched off the vacuum. "I'm coming," she called. And she dashed to the door.

There stood Jason Birchall, carrying a cardboard box. "Hi, Stacy," he said.

"Hi." She was very surprised to see him.

"I've got something to show you," he said. He looked down at whatever was in his box.

She stepped back, away from the door. Jason was known to collect strange pets. Things like tarantulas and croaking bullfrogs.

"Uh . . . I don't know," she said. "Maybe not."

"Come on. Just take a look," he said. "This box won't bite."

"But what's inside might, right?" She didn't trust Jason one bit!

He shoved the cardboard box at her. "Surprise!"

"Yikes!" she gasped.

But it wasn't really so bad when she looked inside.

There was no scary, furry spider. Not even a green frog with blinking eyes!

Instead, a shabby little puppy looked up at her from the box.

"Pee-yew," she said, backing away. "Whose dog?"

154

"That's what *I'd* like to know," he said. "This pooch needs a little kindness. Want to help me hunt for its owner?"

Stacy was shocked. "What did you just say?"

It sounded like Jason had picked a fruit, after all.

"I asked if you wanted to help me find the dog's owner?" he repeated.

"That's very *kind* of you," she replied.

He smiled and set the box down. "I knew you'd think so. But don't get any fruity ideas about . . . well, you know."

She knew, all right.

Still, she hoped Jason would change his mind.

Before New Year's Eve!

# Seven

Sure, I'll help," Stacy agreed. She stooped down and looked into the box. "The poor thing's shivering."

"And that's not all," Jason said. "He needs a bath, too. And I'm not fooling!"

The closer Stacy's nose got to the homeless dog, the more she agreed with Jason. "Bring him inside a minute," she said. "He could get frostbite out here."

Jason nodded. He lifted the box and heaved it into the entryway. "Someone left him on my front step," he explained.

"You're kidding!" Stacy said. "They dropped a puppy off at your house?"

She hated to think of someone being so cruel. She also wondered about the deserted dog. She remembered her feeling earlier today that something wonderful was going to happen to Jason.

"I never saw anyone, either," Jason explained. He seemed very upset. "Muffie just appeared out of nowhere."

"Muffie? You *named* the dog?" Stacy asked.

Jason pushed up his glasses. "Well, I had to call him something. You can't go around with a poor little dog and call him nothing. Can you?"

"Yeah, I guess you're right," Stacy replied. She could hardly believe her ears.

Jason was being very kind! So kind she was sure he'd picked the kindness fruit for the year.

Stacy smiled back at him. "I was just cleaning house," she told him. She eyed the box. "Better keep Muffie in there till I get my jacket."

Jason stooped down and petted the dog. "Hurry, Stacy, it's getting late. My mom said I couldn't be out long," he urged.

Stacy glanced at the window. The sun was setting fast.

Jason was right. They'd have to hurry.

# Eight

**S**tacy rang the doorbell at the first house. A tall man came to the door. "Hey, kids, what's in the box?" the man asked.

Jason didn't waste any time. "Is this your dog, mister?"

The man shook his head. "Sorry," he said and shut the door. *Slam!*

Just up the street from Blossom Hill Lane, they came to the next house.

"You ring, and I'll talk," Stacy said.

"OK," Jason replied. "But get right to the point. People don't want to stand at the door on a cold day."

She agreed. Once again, Jason was thinking of others.

When a pretty lady came to the door, Stacy

asked the question. "We're looking for this darling puppy's owner." She pointed to the box. "Do you know anything about him?" she asked.

The lady peeked into the box. Her mouth dropped open. "What a mess!" she said, then quickly closed the door.

Stacy's teeth were beginning to chatter. "How m-many m-more h-houses?" she asked.

"If you're cold, you should go home," Jason replied. "Muffie's not your problem."

They walked in silence to the next house.

"Do you feel responsible for this dog?" Stacy asked at last.

Jason shrugged. "I'm not out here freezing my ears off for nothing."

"I know," she said. "I think you're doing a wonderful thing."

"Well . . . let's not get carried away," Jason shot back.

He rang the doorbell *and* did the talking this time.

The teenager at the door didn't say a word. Just shook his head and closed the door.

"Is this how Mary and Joseph felt on Christmas Eve?" Jason mumbled.

Stacy's ears prickled. "What did you say?"

"Nothing," Jason said quickly.

But she was pretty sure she'd heard. *Hallelujah!*

■ ■ ■

One after another, they knocked on doors or rang doorbells. Nobody but nobody seemed to know anything about Muffie.

"Well, I guess he's ours," Stacy said.

"Ours?" Jason asked. He turned and gave her an odd look. "What's *that* supposed to mean?"

"Just what I said," she replied.

Then she had another idea. It was perfect! "Maybe Muffie could be our club pet," she suggested. "What do you think of that?"

"I think it stinks," Jason said. "I'm gonna ask my parents if *I* can keep this mystery mutt."

*Mystery mutt?* she thought. *Poor dog!*

Yet she felt the giggles building up inside her. Stacy held them in. Jason would freak if she let them spill out. He hated giggling worse than almost anything.

"Better give Muffie a bath first," she said. "Your mom won't give him a chance, smelling like this."

Jason nodded. "For once, you're right, Stacy Henry."

"Whatever you say," she answered.

"Can I use your bathtub?" he asked.

"*May* you, don't you mean?" Stacy was picky about speech.

Jason blinked his eyes. "Please, not an English lesson now."

"Hey, do that again," she said.

"Do what again?"

"Blink your eyes like your frog," she said. Then the giggles came.

Jason looked like he wanted to run. "C'mon, Stacy. Stop it!"

Stacy tried to be serious. She walked primly and properly to their street, Blossom Hill Lane. All the way, she wondered about Jason. How long before he'd pick a fruit?

162

The fruit of kindness seemed perfect. Or maybe it would be gentleness!

Stacy really hoped he'd pick one, because time was running out. The new year was almost here.

Two days left!

# Nine

Stacy and Jason chattered while they scrubbed the mystery mutt.

"Thanks for letting Muffie use your tub," Jason said.

She'd have to clean the bathroom when Muffie was all done with his doggie bath. And before Mom arrived home.

She enjoyed helping Jason. And he seemed to accept her love and kindness.

"Did you hear? We're having another Cul-de-Sac Kids club meeting," she said.

"When?" Jason asked. Soapsuds were all over his glasses and shirt.

"New Year's Eve," Stacy said. She tried not to giggle at sudsy Jason. But it was hard. He looked so silly.

"What are we gonna do at the meeting?" Jason asked.

A bubble popped on his glasses. It was impossible for Stacy to hold in the giggles now.

"What's so funny?" he said. Jason looked more puzzled than upset.

"You're all soapy." She pointed to his hair and face.

"I am?" He stood up and looked in the mirror. "Hey, you're right. I *do* look funny. Not only funny—I look like a fruit."

Stacy stopped laughing. "What did you say?"

"I'm a prune!" He held up his hands. "Look at me."

Jason was right. He *did* look like a fruit.

She stared down at her own hands. "Wow, I'm wrinkled, too. Just like a girl prune."

Jason went back to washing Muffie.

Stacy helped him dry the dog.

"Muffie's sure cute now. I guess what's in the heart shows up on the outside," said Jason. "Sooner or later."

Stacy was thrilled. But she didn't dare say a word.

"Count me in on the fruity loop." Jason was laughing. Not giggling, but close.

"What's a fruity loop?" she asked.

"You know what a loop is, right?" said Jason.

"I guess so." Stacy wasn't really sure.

"A cul-de-sac is sorta like a loop, isn't it?" Stacy laughed. "Oh, I get it. You're one crazy kid," Stacy said.

"Thanks to the mystery mutt, I'm fruity, too!" replied Jason.

"Now we have to convince your parents to take Muffie," said Stacy.

"Won't be easy," Jason said. "Even with Muffie smelling nice and fresh, my mom's not much for dogs."

"Maybe *my* mom'll let me keep him," she said.

Just then, she heard someone's keys jangle. Stacy looked up. Her mother was standing in the bathroom doorway!

"Oh, hi, Mom," she said. "We needed to give a dog a bath. Hope you don't mind."

Mom frowned. "What's going on?"

"It's a long story," Stacy answered quickly.

"Yes, I suppose it is," Mom said. She came into the room and helped dry Muffie.

"Don't worry, I'll clean things up," Stacy promised.

Mom knelt down and petted the puppy. "Whose dog?"

Stacy looked at Jason.

And Jason looked at Stacy.

They both shrugged at the same time.

"We really don't know," Stacy said at last.

"What do you mean?" Mom asked.

"He's a stray." Jason explained how he'd found him.

"How very sad," Mom said. "But please don't get any ideas about the homeless dog, Stacy."

"I didn't think you'd want *two* dogs," Stacy replied.

Jason pushed up his glasses. "Then it's up to me."

Stacy thought he looked awfully happy. Jason *really* wanted Muffie. She was positively sure!

Stacy helped finish drying the dog—with a hair dryer. Muffie seemed to like the warm air. When he was completely dry, Muffie seemed to smile.

"Look!" Jason said. "Muffie's trying to say thank you."

"Hey, I think you're right," Stacy agreed. She stroked Muffie's white and brown coat.

Sunday Funnies came in and began to whine. He sounded like he was feeling left out.

"Oh, baby," Stacy said, reaching down for her cockapoo. "There's nothing to worry about."

Jason was the one laughing now. "That's right. You're still top dog around here," he teased.

Stacy followed Jason to the front door. "I'll cross my fingers for you," she said.

"Thanks. And say a prayer, too," Jason added.

"I will. I promise," she said.

Stacy could hardly wait to tell Abby!

# Ten

"C"ountdown to midnight!" Stacy shouted.

The Cul-de-Sac Kids were trying very hard to have a meeting at Dunkum's. It was turning into a New Year's Eve party.

"Let's see who can stay awake the longest," Dee Dee said.

"That's easy," Carly said. "I'm a night owl."

"So is Jimmy," Jimmy said, pointing to himself.

"Who else wants to stay up to see the new year?" Abby asked.

"Stacy does," Jason piped up. "Right?"

Stacy wasn't so sure. "Nothing's gonna change, really. There's only one minute's difference between this year and the next."

Abby jumped out of the beanbag chair. "I think it's time for another change," she said.

"Like what?" asked Eric.

"It's time to vote on a new president," Abby said.

"Of the United States?" asked Shawn.

"No, of the Cul-de-Sac Kids," Abby replied. "I've been the president all this year."

"That's OK," Stacy said.

"Yeah, we like it this way," Dunkum said. "We voted you in, and you're stuck."

"Till we vote you out," Dee Dee added with a sly grin.

Everyone laughed at that.

Jason stood up, too. "We'll let you know when we're tired of you, Abby Hunter," he joked.

"Thanks a lot," Abby said.

"Are you giving up so soon?" Carly teased.

Abby smiled a happy smile. "Just wanted to check and make sure," she said.

Jason kept standing. "I have something to say."

Stacy wondered, *What's this about?*

Why was Jason's face so serious?

Was this about the mystery mutt? He'd

seemed so happy since his parents decided to let him keep Muffie.

She was nearly holding her breath.

"I acted real stupid at the last meeting," Jason said.

"Not stupid," Dunkum said. "Nobody thinks that about you."

The other kids were nodding their heads.

"Just listen," Jason said. Stacy could tell he wasn't fooling around. He meant every word. "I picked some fruit this week. Just like the rest of you."

Stacy sighed. This was really wonderful!

Jason kept talking. He wasn't jigging and jiving. He wasn't poking his finger in the air or being a pain. He was doing his best.

"I picked a whole *bunch* of fruit this week," Jason said.

"You did what?" Dee Dee asked.

Jason nodded and grinned. "I picked all nine of them. And I'm gonna see how many I can eat this year."

"Yay!" Everyone was clapping.

The girls jumped up and down.

The boys got up and gave one another high fives.

"Jason's real cool," Stacy said. But nobody heard her. There was so much noise.

"This is double dabble good!" Abby shouted.

Finally, they all sat down again.

All but Jason. He wasn't finished talking. "I want to thank somebody for all this fruity stuff," he said. He was looking at Stacy.

She ducked her head.

"Stacy's idea was never dumb. The fruity loop is real cool!" Jason exclaimed.

"It was God's idea first. Don't forget that," Stacy reminded him.

Carly raised her hand. "I prayed for you, Jason," she said.

"Thanks," he said.

"And you got a new puppy out of the deal," Eric pointed out.

Jason scratched his head. "I can't figure out why my parents let me keep Muffie."

"Because they saw kindness in you," Stacy said.

"And gentleness and joy," added Abby.

"Self-control," said little Jimmy.

"And faithfulness to feed and care for Muffie," said Dunkum.

"Don't forget patience!" Dee Dee and Carly said together.

"Peace, too," said Eric.

"And last, but not least—love," said Stacy.

Shawn nodded his head. "Stacy right."

Stacy looked at her watch. "Guess what? It's the new year!"

"Happy New Year!" Jason was the first to say it.

Stacy was quite sure that it *would* be happy. Very happy.

With God's help!

# BOOK 22

# Big Bad Beans

For my son Jonathan,
who agrees with Jason Birchall
about the "big bad beans."

# One

Jason Birchall pushed through his dresser drawer. He shoved his baseball cards and comic books aside.

His hand bumped the old cardboard box in the corner. His money box! It was the top-secret place where he kept his life savings.

"Jason!" his mother called. "Your after-school snack is ready."

"Super yuck," Jason muttered.

He was tired of his mother's healthy diet. He was even starting to have nightmares about carrots and celery. Last night, three giant carrots had chased him to school!

Jason emptied his jeans pockets. He placed seven dollar bills in a row on his dresser. Then he counted again.

Doing yard work for Stacy Henry's mom was super cool. Only ten more dollars to go. Soon, Eric Hagel's mountain bike would belong to him.

*Yahoo!* Jason could hardly wait.

He folded the seven dollar bills. Then he stuffed them into his money box.

Hiding the box was a smart thing to do. He pushed it way back, into the corner of the drawer.

Suddenly, he spied a pack of bubble gum. His mouth began to water. He could almost taste the sweet, gooey gum.

How long had it been since he'd chewed bubble gum?

Weeks ago, his mother had read a silly health-food book. *"Time for some big changes,"* she'd said.

Maybe the diet was OK for her and Dad, but Jason wanted sweets. He wadded up four pieces of bubble gum and smashed them into his mouth.

"Jason, dear," Mom called again.

*Phooey!*

The bubble gum had to go. But Jason didn't

want to swallow it. That would be a waste. He would save the sugary wad for later.

Quickly, he stuck the gum on the wrapper. And—*wham!*—he closed the drawer.

*Safe!*

"I'm coming." He hurried to his bedroom door.

His mother was standing in the hallway, holding a tray of sliced carrots and celery sticks.

"Double yuck." Jason wrinkled up his face at the orange and green vegetables.

"Aren't you hungry?" Mom asked, inching the tray closer.

"Not for this stuff," he said.

"Have you been snitching sweets?" she asked.

Jason shook his head no. He had stuck to the diet. Anyway, gum didn't count.

His mother smiled. "This snack will do you good."

Jason shrugged. He took a handful of the orange and green health sticks.

When his mother left, he pulled the junk drawer open again. There he found his wad of bubble gum. He sniffed the strawberry flavor.

*Yum!* His favorite!

Jason looked at the carrots and celery sticks in his hand. "Better stay out of my dreams tonight," he warned.

Then he gobbled the raw vegetables down—to get it over with. He couldn't wait to get the horrible taste out of his mouth.

He reached for the wad of bubble gum and stuffed his face. Jason tiptoed to the bedroom door and peeked out. All clear! Mom was nowhere in sight.

Fast as a super spider, he tiptoed down the hall to the front door. Time to visit Eric Hagel next door. And time to check out the flashy mountain bike.

*Soon it'll be mine!* thought Jason.

# TWO

Jason ran next door to Eric's house. He nearly stumbled over Stacy Henry. She was sitting near the driveway, staring at some black ants.

"Hey, Stacy," he said. "What are you doing?"

"Nothing much." She looked up. "What are *you* doing?"

"I have to talk to Eric," he told her.

"He's busy cleaning out the garage." She pointed toward the house. "In there."

Jason hurried up the driveway and leaned against the side of the garage door. "Looks like you're working too hard," he teased.

Eric stopped sweeping. "What's up?"

Jason wandered in and looked around. "How clean does your garage have to be?"

"Clean enough to earn my allowance," Eric replied.

"Looks good to me," Jason said.

Eric laughed. "Tell my mom that."

Jason spotted the mountain bike. It was parked in the corner of the garage. "When are you getting your *new* bike?" he asked.

"Next week, if you come up with the money for my old one," Eric explained.

Jason danced around. "I only need ten more bucks," he said.

"That's a lot," Eric said. "Where are you gonna get it?"

Jason shrugged. "Beats me, but I will!"

He turned and watched Stacy. She was letting ants crawl over her fingers on the sunny cement. "Hey, Stacy," he called. "Does your mom need any more help in her garden?"

"Don't think so," Stacy replied.

"Maybe Abby Hunter can give you some ideas," Eric said. "The president of the Cul-de-Sac Kids oughta be able to think of something, right?"

Jason laughed. "Me, work with a girl?"

"You helped my mom," Stacy spoke up. "*She's* a girl."

"That's different," Jason muttered. He eyed Eric's bike and moved toward it.

*Just ten more bucks*, he thought. He touched the shiny frame. The golden flecks shone through the royal blue. It was easy to imagine himself speeding down Blossom Hill Lane. "I have to have this bike," he whispered. "Have to!"

"It's yours when you cough up the money," Eric reminded him.

Jason was startled. Eric had heard him.

"Well, I'll see you later," Jason said.

He crossed the street to Abby's house. Her father was outside shooting baskets. Mr. Hunter tossed the ball to Jason.

"Is Abby home?" Jason asked.

"She's shopping with her mother," Mr. Hunter said.

Jason turned and shot. He made a basket on the first try.

Across the street, Eric hopped on his old bike. He flew past Abby's house and down the street.

Jason watched him go. "Where's *he* headed?" he whispered.

He aimed the ball and shot. It bounced off the rim.

Just then, Mr. Hunter's pager beeped. With a smile, he waved to Jason and rushed inside.

Jason stood holding the basketball. He didn't like the idea of waiting around for Abby. Why couldn't *he* think of a way to earn the extra money?

■■■

At supper, Jason poked at the salad on his plate. He played with his lettuce and sprouts. He glared at the garbanzo beans. "Why must we eat these big, bad beans?" he whined.

"They're good for you," his mother said. "That's why."

"But they stick in my throat," he argued.

His father spoke up. "You might try chewing them, son."

Jason tried, but it was no use. The beans tasted horrible. And they were too big to swallow whole, like a pill.

He waited till his parents weren't looking. Then he sneaked some beans to Muffie. His new puppy would eat them. He loved people food. Any kind!

Just then the doorbell rang.

Jason leaped from the table.

There stood Eric at the front door. "I've gotta tell you something," Eric said. Then he flipped the kickstand down on the blue mountain bike.

"What's up?" Jason asked.

Eric scratched his head. He was acting strange. "Someone else wants to buy my bike. He'll give me five more bucks than you."

Jason felt his neck grow warm. "Is that where you zoomed off to today? To sell your bike to someone else?"

Eric's wide eyes blinked three times. "Yeah, guess so," he said.

"But . . . we had a deal," Jason pleaded. His breath was coming fast. "You can't change your mind now!"

Eric stared at Jason. "Well, can you match his offer?"

"You want more money?" Jason asked.

"Here's the deal." Eric rubbed his fingers together. "Whoever's first with the bucks gets the bike."

Jason stared at the super-cool bike. "I'm already ten dollars short," he muttered.

"Too bad, then." Eric turned to go.

The lump in his throat made Jason cough. "There's just no way," he said.

# Three

Jason marched over to Abby's the next day. He told her his plan to buy Eric's mountain bike. And he told her about Eric's rotten deal.

Abby shook her head. "Sounds like you need some quick money. I know just the thing—a recycling project."

"A what?" Jason asked.

"You know, a recycling project. Care for the earth and pick up some extra cash at the same time. I'll call the other Cul-de-Sac Kids to help," she said.

"Yahoo!" shouted Jason. "When do we start?"

Abby sat on the porch step. "Tomorrow's Saturday. Meet me in front of my house at eight."

"Gotcha." Jason raced home to count the money in his box. One more time.

■■■

Saturday morning, Jason met Abby in front of her house.

Dee Dee Winters and Abby's little sister, Carly, pulled wagons. Stacy Henry wore her mother's garden gloves.

Dunkum Mifflin showed up with armloads of trash bags. Abby and Carly's Korean brothers, Shawn and Jimmy, helped carry the bags.

Jason smiled. He felt good having so many friends. Cul-de-Sac Kid friends!

Only Eric was missing.

But Jason didn't care. He'd show Eric all about good deals. He'd have the money soon. Maybe even today!

"If you buy Eric's mountain bike, I'll race you," Dee Dee teased.

"We sure will!" Carly piped up.

Jason pushed up his glasses. He had more important things on his mind than bike races. At least for now.

Dunkum whistled with his fingers. "We'll

stop at every house in the cul-de-sac. Then all the houses up the street from the school. Abby, Stacy, and I will gather newspapers. Carly and Dee Dee can pull the glass bottles in the wagons. Jason, you, Shawn, and Jimmy can collect aluminum cans." Dunkum gave Jason a handful of heavy-duty trash bags. "We'll split the money evenly," he said.

"Super good," Jason said.

Abby grinned. "Let's go to Eric's house first," she suggested.

"Hooray!" the kids agreed.

"This is a fun way to earn money," Dee Dee said.

Carly hurried to catch up with Dee Dee.

Shawn and Jimmy Hunter chattered in Korean.

Abby, Stacy, and Dunkum told jokes.

Jason jigged and jived.

By lunchtime, the kids had gathered a mountain of recyclable items. Enough to fill Abby's father's van.

Jason, Abby, and Dunkum rode along to the recycling center.

On the way back, Jason counted his share

of the money. Fifteen dollars and forty-eight cents' worth of work.

*Yes!* He ran across the street to Eric's.

No one was home.

*Phooey*, he thought.

Eager to buy the bike, Jason darted home. He went to his room and counted *all* his money for the last time.

Jason wanted to dance. There was plenty of money to buy Eric's bike!

■ ■ ■

At lunch, he ate fish and salad without fussing. But he nearly choked on the garbanzo beans. He excused himself every few minutes to see if Eric was home yet.

His mom went to the kitchen for more herbal tea.

His dad reached for the TV remote and turned on the Weather Channel.

Quickly, Jason offered his last garbanzo bean to Muffie. The puppy chomped it right down.

*Yahoo!*

Jason didn't bother to excuse himself from the table. He hurried off to his room.

There, he rooted through his junk drawer. *Gotta have some strawberry bubble gum*, he thought.

Just then, he heard someone drive up at Eric's.

"Yes!" He grabbed his money and slammed the drawer. The bubble gum would just have to wait again.

Eric's grandpa was pulling into the garage when Jason arrived. Jason waited for Eric and his grandpa to get out of the car.

"I've got the money," Jason shouted, waving it in Eric's face. "Even the extra five bucks!"

Eric seemed to smirk. "Too late," he said.

Jason stared at Eric in the dimly lit garage. He was too stunned to speak.

Eric dug his hand into his pocket. He waved a bunch of dollar bills. "Sorry, someone beat you to it," he said.

"No way!" Jason shouted. "That's not fair!"

"A deal's a deal," Eric said. Then he turned and trudged into the house.

Jason wanted to holler and carry on.

But it was no use.

# Four

Jason slipped in through the back door of his house. He tiptoed down the hall to his room. The floor squeaked on the way.

"Jason, is that you?" his mother called from the living room.

*Rats!* She'd want him to eat another healthy snack.

What *he* wanted was to chew up three packs of bubble gum. Right now, he wished he had two hundred packs of gum.

"Jason?" came his mother's voice again.

He looked at the clock. "Time for the carrot and celery brigade," he whispered.

Sure enough, here came Mom with a full tray.

Jason picked out two skinny celery sticks

and three short carrot sticks. He waited till his mother left the room. Then he lifted his mattress and stuffed the orange and green sticks underneath.

"That's where veggie sticks belong," he muttered.

Then he headed for his junk drawer. He could almost taste his yummy strawberry bubble gum!

■ ■ ■

The next morning, Jason watched Abby Hunter's family climb into their van. Every Sunday, they attended church, always together.

Stacy Henry, Abby's best friend, was going along. So was Dunkum Mifflin, the best hoop shooter around. And little Dee Dee Winters. Seven Cul-de-Sac Kids, counting the Hunter kids.

*They could almost have a club meeting,* thought Jason with a sigh.

Abby often asked Jason to go with them. Dunkum did, too.

But Jason gave her plenty of excuses. For one thing, he wasn't used to going to church.

For another, his dress-up clothes were too small.

"None of that matters," Abby always said. "God just wants us to show up."

But Jason refused to go.

After the van left, he wandered outside. He sat on the front step and stared at Eric's house. *The lousy double-crosser better stay inside all day*, he thought.

Hey! Now, Eric—*there* was a kid for Sunday school and church!

■■■

The Hunters' van arrived back around noon.

Jason was still sitting on the step, bored silly.

Abby ran across the street. "Hi, Jason."

"What's up?" he asked.

"Plenty," she said, out of breath. "Can you hide something for me?"

Jason pushed up his glasses. "Maybe."

Abby opened her purse. She pulled out a sandwich bag full of dollar bills.

"Wow," said Jason. "That's a bunch of money."

"Sh-h! It's for Mother's Day," Abby whispered. "And it's top secret."

"Really?"

She handed the plastic money bag to him. "I can't seem to hide this anymore. I think someone's found my hiding place."

"Like who?"

"I'm not sure," Abby replied.

Jason clutched her bag of bills. "Your bucks are safe with me!"

"Double dabble good!" She turned to cross the street. "Thanks, Jason."

"How long should I hide the you-know-what?" Jason called to her.

"I'll need it next Saturday. Dad and I are going shopping for Mother's Day," Abby said. "But don't tell anyone. OK?"

Jason nodded. "It's a done deal."

Abby smiled. "Thanks again." She turned to go but stopped in the middle of the street. "How's the bike deal coming?" she asked.

Suddenly, Jason felt sick. "Oh, that," he said.

Abby frowned hard. "What's wrong?"

Jason sat stone still. Should he tell on Eric?

"C'mon, Jason. Did you buy the bike or not?" she asked.

"Eric double-crossed me," he blurted.

Abby's eyes nearly popped out. "You're kidding . . . how?"

"He sold the bike out from under my nose," Jason said.

He felt horrible as soon as he said it.

Worse than ever!

# Five

Jason wished Abby would stop staring at him. He could see she wasn't leaving. Not until he explained.

"Eric sold his bike to someone else," he repeated. "That's all there is to it."

Abby sighed. "This is double dabble rotten."

"It's not your fault," he said.

Abby sat beside him on the step. "I can't believe this."

"He's a double-crosser, that's what," Jason said.

Abby nodded her head. "No kidding."

Dunkum came up the street just then. He was dribbling his basketball. "Wanna play?" he asked Jason.

"Not today," Jason replied.

Dunkum stopped bouncing the ball. He looked first at Jason, then at Abby. "Who died?" he asked.

"Nobody," Abby said. But her face looked all droopy.

"Could have fooled me," Dunkum said. He twirled the basketball on his finger. "Come on, Jason, let's shoot some hoops."

"Don't feel like it," Jason replied.

Dunkum raised his eyebrows. "Why not?"

Abby stood up. "I better get going," she said.

"See you," Jason called.

Dunkum and Jason headed for the far end of the street. It was the dead end of the cul-de-sac. A grassy place with a large oak tree, near Mr. Tressler's house.

Dunkum leaned against the old tree. He tossed his basketball to the ground. "What's going on?" he asked.

"Don't ask," Jason said.

Dunkum frowned and let the subject drop. He pulled a black book from his back pocket. "Check this out," he said.

Jason sat on the ground, eyeing the tiny book. "What is it?"

"It's a New Testament. I got it the first time I went to Abby's church." He paused for a second. "I've learned lots of verses from it."

"What's so great about that?" Jason asked.

Dunkum grinned. "If I say all the verses by next Sunday, I'll win another ribbon. Then I'll have twenty-five. Maybe I'll even win the grand prize!"

Jason didn't give a hoot about church prizes. He was thinking about the bike that got away.

"Here," Dunkum said. He handed the pocket Bible to Jason. "Follow along and see if I've got my verses right. OK?"

"Whatever," Jason mumbled. "If you *have* to."

So Dunkum began.

Halfway through the first verse, Jason stopped him. "Wrong. You're mixed up," he said.

Dunkum started over. But he missed more words.

"You were real close." Jason closed the book. "I oughta go home now. Mom's leafy lunch is calling."

Dunkum nodded. "Thanks. Can you help me again?" he asked.

"Maybe," Jason said, getting up. He wiped his hands on his jeans.

They hurried down Blossom Hill Lane. Jason pushed his hand deep into his pants pocket. Yes! Abby's money was safe there.

"Wanna come to church next Sunday?" asked Dunkum. "It's Mother's Day. Bring your mom and get a rose."

Jason scratched his head. "She'd like that."

They walked past Eric's house. Jason looked the other way on purpose.

"See you later," Dunkum said. He darted across the street. The basketball danced under one leg. "Come over Wednesday after school," he called. "I'll have my verses ready by then."

"I guess so," said Jason. He didn't see what was so special about saying Bible verses from memory. Except maybe for the grand prize. Whatever *that* was.

After lunch, he went to his room and opened his junk drawer. Abby's cash fit into his cardboard money box. He stacked up a pile of baseball cards between her money and his. Abby's Mother's Day money was on the left and his money was on the right.

*Super good!*

Now . . . he needed to find another used bike to buy. Everything would be good again if he could.

Quickly, Jason emptied his other pocket. Big, bad garbanzo beans were inside. He'd sneaked them off his plate at lunch.

Surely Mom could come up with something better than yucky bean salads. But if not, he'd have to hide them in his junk drawer. They'd be fine there until trash day.

Wednesday!

# Six

It was Monday.

Jason's class lined up for art. They were making pop-up heart vases from construction paper for Mother's Day.

Eric put glue bottles on each table. When he passed Jason's table, he bragged about his new mountain bike. "I'm getting it in two days," he said.

Jason felt sick again. All the Cul-de-Sac Kids had cool bikes. Even Dee Dee Winters.

Abby sat across from him at the table. She was helping the new girl follow the pattern, fold, and cut the pages.

Jason watched her do what she did best— help others. He wanted to thank her for helping him raise money for Eric's bike. Eric's dumb old mountain bike. The one he never got to buy!

The word was out by morning recess that Eric had double-crossed Jason. Everyone knew about it. Even the little kids!

Bossy Dee Dee warned Jason about buying chocolate bars with his leftover bike money. "You'll spoil your mom's plans for your health," she teased.

"Mind your own business." He turned away to find a soccer game.

"It's not the only bike in the world," Dee Dee said.

Maybe to her it wasn't. But Dee Dee hadn't felt the smooth, shiny frame, or seen its golden flecks smiling through the blue. She hadn't heard the whir of its jazzy tire spokes.

*Brr-i-i-ing!* The bell rang.

Everyone raced to the school. Everyone except Jason. He dragged his feet.

■■■

After school on Wednesday, Jason went straight home.

He tossed pieces of lettuce and three wrinkled garbanzo beans from his lunch into the junk drawer. His money and Abby's money were safely hidden in the corner.

Then he headed to Dunkum's house. Time to help him practice Bible verses.

Dunkum stood tall beside his desk.

Jason sat on the bed, checking the words in the New Testament.

"Galations 6:2: 'Carry each other's burdens, and in this way you will fulfill the law of Christ.'"

"You said it perfectly!" said Jason. "Now what?"

"Luke 3:11: 'Anyone who has two shirts should share with the one who has none, and anyone who has food should do the same.'"

"That's correct." Jason handed the New Testament back. "Wow, I didn't know the Bible said stuff like that."

"Me either," said Dunkum. "Not till I found out at Abby's church." He headed for the garage.

Jason followed. "So are you gonna do it?"

"Do what?" Dunkum reached for his basketball.

"You know, share some *real* food with me. Like it says in the Bible," Jason said.

"Oh no, you don't." Dunkum shot two baskets. "I won't be responsible for messing with your mom's diet."

"But it's a real yucky diet. Garbanzo beans and lettuce—junk like that. Nobody knows how horrible it is." Jason sat on an old bench in the corner. He watched Dunkum do his fancy footwork.

*Zing!* The ball went right in. Perfect shot.

"Your turn," Dunkum said.

"Are you going to win the grand prize at church on Sunday?" Jason asked.

"Hope so," Dunkum answered. He whirled around and swished the ball through the hoop.

"What's the prize?" Jason asked.

"Hot new Rollerblades," Dunkum said, out of breath.

"Really?" He bounced the ball and took a shot. In it went!

"That's what I'm trying for," Dunkum said. "I'm tired of riding my bikes anyway. Playing ball is *my* thing. But blading . . . I could practice basketball on them."

Jason stopped bouncing the ball. "Did you say *bikes*? You got more than one?"

"Sure. You remember my old road bike. Plus, my dad bought me a brand-new BMX. I hardly ever ride them anymore," Dunkum said.

"How come?" Jason couldn't believe his ears.

"Basketball is my life." Dunkum fired one up. The ball swished right through. Nothing but net!

At that moment, Jason had a new idea. He took a deep breath. "Want to sell one of your bikes?"

Dunkum stopped. He wiped his face on his sleeve. "Hey, good idea. The road bike needs some paint. That's all."

"Yahoo!" shouted Jason. "How much?"

"Whatever you got," Dunkum said. He dribbled the ball behind his back.

"Don't go away!" Jason hurried home to get the money. He could trust Dunkum any day. He was not a double-crosser.

# Seven

J ason flew to his room.

The place was a mess. Pajamas and towels were crumpled in a heap in the corner. The bed was lumpy. His dresser drawers yawned open, and jeans played peekaboo over the top.

He kicked away pieces of gum wrapper with his foot.

Gum wrappers?

What were *they* doing out?

He scrambled to his knees and pushed the comic books aside. The junk drawer was junkier than ever!

Searching, he found his bike money in the back of the drawer. The baseball cards divided his money on the right from Abby's on the . . .

"What's this?" he wailed.

Abby's money was all ripped up! Bits of garbanzo beans were mixed in with shredded dollar bills.

"What happened?" Jason cried. "Who did this?"

A trail of the scrappy mess led to the bathroom. He found his puppy whining in the corner of the shower.

"Bad, bad Muffie!" He wanted to shake him. No, that was too kind. He wanted to hang Muffie up by his doggie ears.

"How could you do this?" he shouted.

Muffie yipped and backed farther into the shower stall.

Jason slammed the bathroom door and looked in the mirror. He yelled at his own face. "Can't you do *anything* right?"

He slapped himself on the forehead. "It was those big, bad beans!" Jason exclaimed. "I should have known . . . I should have . . ."

His mother knocked on the door. "Jason, are you all right?"

"I'm doomed. Abby's money is all gone! Muffie ate it!" he said over and over.

"I can't understand you," Mom said.

"Everything's wrong," he muttered. "Abby counted on me and now . . ."

He picked Muffie out of the shower. His breath smelled like beans. "You little sneak," he hollered in the pooch's face. "I should never have let you live here!"

Poor little Muffie shook in his arms. He carried him to the back door and put him out. Then he slammed the kitchen door and headed for his room.

The junk drawer was sagging open. Half a garbanzo bean and some lettuce were scattered in the front—the reason for Muffie's mischief.

But deep inside, Jason knew it was his own fault.

He groaned. *Those good-for-nothing beans! If only I'd cleaned my plate.*

Just then, the doorbell rang.

"Jason," called his mother. "Your friend Abby's here to see you."

His heart sank. Abby had come early for

her Mother's Day money. He was almost positive!

Jason breathed fast and hard. How much money had she given him? How many dollar bills?

On the floor behind the door, he spied the sandwich baggie. The amount was written on a round pink sticker.

Twenty-two dollars!

Jason gasped. What could he do?

Quickly, he counted his own money. It was all there.

He thought about Dunkum's terrific road bike down the street, just waiting to be his!

But he had no choice. Jason stuffed his own money into the sandwich bag. He would give it all to Abby Hunter. She'd never know what happened to her half-eaten money. Or worse—that he couldn't be counted on.

He shuffled down the hall. No bike for a kid with a health-food freak for a dog!

"I'm coming, Abby," he called.

Jason tried to swallow the lump in his throat. It was very hard.

# Eight

**B**rr-i-i-ing! The phone rang right after Abby left.

Jason ran to get it. "Hello," he said.

"Where *are* you?" Dunkum asked. "I thought you were coming back to buy my road bike."

"I was, but . . ." Jason stopped. "Mom is real sick and she needs me here." It was a lie.

"Sorry about that," Dunkum said. "Tomorrow after school, then?"

"Uh . . . no. I can't come then, either." Jason quickly made up another story. "Abby and I are working on a science project."

"What project?" Dunkum asked.

"I . . . I . . . uh, have to go," Jason said.

He stared at the phone and felt lousy. He'd lied to Dunkum. Twice!

■ ■ ■

The next day, Jason avoided Dunkum at morning recess.

But Dunkum cornered him in the afternoon. "You're acting weird," Dunkum said. "How come?"

Jason's face felt hot. His hands were sweaty. "I guess I don't tell lies very well," he confessed.

"You lied to me?" Dunkum looked puzzled. "About what?"

Jason stumbled over his words. "I lied . . . about . . . about why I didn't buy your bike."

"You did?"

He didn't want to tell Dunkum about Muffie eating Abby's money. He didn't want Abby to find out. She would think he couldn't be counted on. That would be horrible!

"It's a long story," Jason said. "You'd never believe it anyway."

"That's OK," said Dunkum. "You don't have to buy my bike if you don't want to. I just thought . . ."

"But I *do* want to buy it. More than any-thing," Jason said.

"So . . . what's the problem?" Dunkum asked.

Jason thought about it. Should he spill the beans?

"I'll tell you if you keep it quiet," he said at last.

Dunkum nodded. "I won't tell. Scout's honor."

"No fooling?" Jason begged for a promise.

"No fooling," Dunkum said.

Jason told the truth this time. Every bit of it.

Dunkum stared at him. "You're kidding. You used your own money so Abby wouldn't know hers got eaten by Muffie?"

Jason pulled out his pocket linings. "See? I'm broke," he said.

"Let me get this straight," Dunkum said. "You gave Abby the money you made from our recycling project? The bucks that were gonna buy you some cool wheels?"

"It wasn't easy, but that's the *real* story," Jason said.

"Wow! That is some act of charity," Dunkum said.

"Huh?" Jason pushed up his glasses.

"Charity. You know . . . kindness. When you give because you care." Dunkum pushed his hair back.

Jason laughed. "Sounds like a Mother's Day card."

"Hey, no kidding. We talked about that in Sunday school last week," Dunkum said.

"Really? You talk about stuff like that?" Jason asked.

"Sure. Have you ever heard this before: 'It is better to give than to receive'?" Dunkum was grinning.

Jason snapped his fingers. "Some wise old saying, right?"

Dunkum nodded. "Better than wise. It's in the Bible."

"Mixed in with those verses about sharing food?" Jason asked.

Dunkum laughed out loud.

"Gotcha," teased Jason.

Dunkum's smile faded. "See you at church this Sunday?" he asked.

"If I come, will you say your verses? About

sharing and feeding kids on yucky diets?"
added Jason. "I wouldn't want to miss that."

"You bet!" Dunkum seemed pleased. "And
remember: Bring your mom and get a rose."

The school bell rang.

Jason and Dunkum hurried inside.

Jason felt super great. He wondered how
he could pass a feeling like this on to Eric,
the double-crosser. The new mountain-bike
owner, the rotten . . .

No, he wouldn't even think that. He'd keep
his thoughts to himself.

Miss Hershey stood up. She gave the math
assignment. "Class, please turn to page 118,"
she said. "Begin by solving problem number
one. And be sure to show your work."

Jason could hardly believe his eyes. The
math problem was about four boys in a mar-
athon bike race.

A mountain-bike race!

# Nine

What a sunny Mother's Day!

Jason's dad was on a business trip. So Jason and his mom attended Abby's church together. The pastor gave them each a small New Testament, just like Dunkum's.

Jason crossed his fingers when Dunkum said his verses. After Dunkum was finished, Jason said, "You did it! Go, Dunkum!"

Abby clapped her hands. "Dunkum's double dabble good!"

Jason thought Abby was pretty cool, too. For a girl, of course.

"Now for the grand prize," Abby whispered. She took her place beside Dunkum and three others.

Dunkum was up against four girls!

Jason listened to each verse. And he decided something right then. The Bible verses were much better than just wise old sayings. He looked down at his New Testament. Carefully, he held it with both hands.

Soon, the first round was finished.

*Whew, that was close!* thought Jason. He really hoped Dunkum would win.

Next, it was Abby's turn. She was super at saying her verses. *She oughta be,* he thought. Abby had been doing this all her life.

Things were much different for Dunkum. He was new at this.

At last, the final round came.

The girls wrinkled their noses or twisted their hair before reciting each verse.

One girl forgot the chapter and verse but said the book of the Bible. She was out.

Her mistake was catching. The other girls forgot a word, too.

Dunkum looked very relaxed. Was he thinking about basketball or the grand prize? Or both?

Squeezing his New Testament, Jason rooted for Dunkum. He felt like cheering or dancing. But he sat quietly, hard as it was.

"Dunkum Mifflin," the teacher said. "Please say Luke 3:11."

Dunkum paused. He glanced at the ceiling.

Jason watched and waited. *C'mon, you can do it*, he thought.

Even Jason remembered this verse. It was the good one about sharing junk food with a kid on a health diet.

The teacher looked at her stopwatch. "Five seconds to go."

Jason's heart leaped up.

The air was tense. The suspense was too much.

Just as the teacher started to raise her hand, Dunkum began, "'Anyone who has two shirts should share with the one who has none, and anyone who has food should do the same.' Luke 3:11," he said.

Jason sighed.

Abby was next. It looked like she was holding her breath. Jason couldn't tell for sure.

The teacher said another verse. Abby had to tell where it was found—the backward approach.

*Very tricky*, thought Jason.

There was a long silence.

Abby turned to Dunkum. "I don't think I know that one," she admitted.

"You have five seconds," the teacher said again.

Abby looked up. She looked down. She shook her folded hands.

"Time's up" came the teacher's voice.

Dunkum was the grand-prize winner! Everyone clapped for both Dunkum and Abby.

Abby was the second-place winner. Her eyes danced as she shook Dunkum's hand.

*What a good sport!* thought Jason. He shot her a thumbs-up.

"Thanks, Jason," Abby said as she sat down.

Dunkum took a seat beside him. "Abby's a winner at losing," Dunkum whispered. "Get it?"

"She sure is. Now what?" Jason asked.

"The grand prize!" said Dunkum.

Jason stood up and did a quick jig. He just had to!

# Ten

After church, Jason opened the car door for Dunkum. He helped load Dunkum's grand prize into the van.

On the ride home, they checked out the slick new Rollerblades.

Abby and her little sister, Carly, leaned over the seat for a closer look. Her brothers, Shawn and Jimmy, looked, too.

"Wow! Your Rollerblades are double dabble terrific!" said Abby.

"How many verses total?" Abby's father asked Dunkum.

Dunkum grinned. "Twenty-five," he said.

"Amazing," said Jason's mom. She was holding *two* Mother's Day roses.

Jason's stomach was beginning to growl.

He excused the rumble. "Sorry . . . I'm just hungry," he said.

His mother's face beamed. "There's a surprise in the oven."

"Real food, I hope?" asked Jason.

"How does meatloaf sound for a change?" she said.

"Yahoo!"

Dunkum stuffed his fancy Rollerblades back in the box. "I've been thinking, Jason. What if I just *give* you my road bike?"

Jason couldn't believe his ears. "You'd do that?" he said.

"Sure . . . why not?" Dunkum pushed the lid down. "I've got what I want right here." He tapped on the box. "And in here." He patted his chest.

"You've gotta be kidding," Jason said.

"The verses aren't just in my head anymore. They're in my heart, too," Dunkum explained.

Jason held his New Testament real tight. He was beginning to understand what Dunkum meant.

Dunkum tapped his fingers on the grand-prize box. "Luke 3:11—*my* way—says: If you have two bikes, which I do, share with Jason, who doesn't have even one."

Abby was laughing. "Dunkum would make a good preacher," she said.

Blossom Hill Lane came into view. The van turned the corner to the cul-de-sac.

Jason jittered, eager to get out. "This was some cool Mother's Day," he said.

His mother smiled. "Thank you for inviting us," she told Abby's parents.

"You're welcome any time." Abby had a sparkle in her eye.

"How about next Sunday?" asked Jason.

"Hooray!" cheered Dunkum, climbing out of the van. "Hey, come over after dinner and pick up your new bike."

Jason's mother smiled. "Better check with your parents first," she said.

"I will," Dunkum said and hurried home.

Jason crossed the street with his mother. "Happy Mother's Day, Mom," he said.

"Thanks, Jason." She smelled the roses, then handed him one. "Is there a reason why we got *two* roses?" she asked. There was a twinkle in her eye.

Jason held the front door open. He smelled

the meatloaf cooking inside. "No big, bad beans today?" he asked.

She smiled. "It's time for another change."

"Yes!" Jason shouted and headed for Eric's house.

■■■

Next door was noisy. Eric's grandpa was mowing the lawn.

Eric was in the garage, shining the spokes on his new bike.

Jason felt uneasy. He held out a long-stemmed rose. "Hi, Eric," he said.

"What's the rose for?" Eric asked.

"Give it to your mom for Mother's Day," Jason said.

"Hey, thanks." Eric looked surprised. Really surprised. "Where'd it come from?"

"Abby's church gave roses to all the mothers," he said.

"That's cool," Eric said.

Jason was dying to ask Eric something. Finally, he did. "How do you like your new bike?"

Eric shrugged his shoulders. "It's OK, but I miss my old one."

"You do?"

"I wish I'd kept it. Or sold it to *you*," Eric said. "It's already a piece of junk. You would have taken better care of it."

Jason didn't know what to say. Before today, he might have felt secretly glad. Glad that Eric messed up by selling his bike to someone else.

Not today. Things were different.

"Well, I've gotta go," Jason said.

"What's your hurry?" Eric asked and stood up.

"Got a lunch date with my mom," Jason told him.

"For Mother's Day?" asked Eric. He held the rose stem carefully between two thorns.

"Yep. She makes a mean meatloaf," he said.

"Sounds like total yuck," Eric muttered.

Jason didn't mind. Meatloaf sure did beat out garbanzo beans any day.

And bikes? Dunkum owned two of them. And thanks to Luke 3:11, one would be Jason's.

*Yahoo!*

# BOOK 23

# The Upside-Down Day

School SPIRIT

To Amy, my niece,
who once played a trick
on Barbara Birch's fourth-grade class
at Pike's Peak Elementary School.

# One

School Spirit Day was coming to Blossom Hill School.

"We're going to have so much fun," said Abby Hunter. She and her friend Stacy Henry hurried down the cul-de-sac together.

Stacy grinned. "I've got *lots* of school spirit," she said.

"Remember the fun we had last year?" said Abby.

"Sure do," Stacy said, skipping along.

"The teachers did real silly things," Abby said.

"I wonder what Miss Hershey will do," Stacy said.

Abby was sure Miss Hershey would make

things interesting. "I can't wait to find out," she replied.

■■■

The Cul-de-Sac Kids walked to school together every day, rain or shine.

But today, something was different.

Abby noticed a girl sitting on Dunkum Mifflin's porch swing. She had long brown hair. Her eyes were closed, and a golden Labrador retriever sat nearby. "Who's that?" Abby whispered to Stacy.

Stacy shook her head. "I've never seen her before."

Abby wondered. "Is she asleep on Dunkum's porch?" she asked more softly.

"I can't tell if she's asleep or not," Stacy replied.

Abby inched closer. "Hello?" she called to the girl.

"Hello, yourself," the girl said. But her eyes were still closed. "You're Abby Hunter, right?"

*How does she know?* Abby wondered.

"Wow! How did you *do* that?" Stacy blurted out.

The girl's eyes opened, but they stared straight ahead. "Dunkum said you'd show up soon. That's how."

Abby looked at the girl. She looked at the dog. She looked back at the girl. *She's blind*, Abby decided. *And whoever she is, she knows Dunkum. But . . . she can't see.*

"What's *your* name?" asked Abby.

"Ellen Mifflin. I'm Dunkum's cousin. This is my guide dog, Honey."

"So . . . are you visiting Dunkum?" Abby asked.

"I'm staying for a couple of months. My dad is overseas for his job."

"Hey, that's great," Abby said. "We need more girls in the Cul-de-Sac Kids club."

"Sure do!" agreed Stacy.

"What's a Cul-de-Sac Kids club?" asked Ellen.

"Well, we live on a cul-de-sac. So we have a club of kids from the cul-de-sac," Abby explained.

"Sounds like fun," said Ellen. "How many girls?"

"Counting you, there are five. You, me, my sister, Carly, Dee Dee Winters, and Stacy

Henry." Abby pulled her friend closer. "Stacy's right here beside me."

"Hi, Stacy," said Ellen with a smile.

"Welcome to Blossom Hill Lane," Stacy said.

Just then, Dunkum leaped out the door. He aimed his basketball at the hoop. He shot. *Swish*. Right through!

"Hi, Abby and Stacy. Did you meet my cousin?" He dribbled the ball behind his back. He loved to show off.

"Sure did," Abby said. "Why didn't you tell us she was coming?"

"You needed another mystery to solve," Dunkum said.

Abby grinned. Dunkum knew she liked a good mystery.

"Speaking of mysteries, are you finished reading *Mystery History* yet?" Abby asked Dunkum.

"Is that all you care about—reading and writing?" Dunkum teased.

"That, and solving mysteries—don't forget!" Abby added. "So, did you finish my book or not?"

"Yep, I'll go get it for you." Dunkum disappeared into the house.

Ellen giggled. "Dunkum forgets stuff. I bet that's why he forgot to tell you I was coming."

The girls laughed. Ellen was right.

In a flash, Dunkum was back with Abby's book.

Just then, someone down the street hollered, "Wait for us!"

Abby turned to look. The rest of the Cul-de-Sac Kids were on their way.

"Here come the rest of the kids," said Abby.

Abby's little sister, Carly, and little brother, Jimmy, ran down the sidewalk toward them. "Nice doggie!" Carly cried when she spied Honey.

"Ellen, meet my sister and brother, Carly and Jimmy," said Abby.

"Hi, Ellen, what's your doggie's name?" Carly asked.

"Hi, Carly." Ellen laughed. "I call my dog Honey."

"I like puppy dogs," said Jimmy, inching close to Honey.

Eric Hagel came running, too. "Better hurry, or we'll be late for school," he said.

"Relax, Eric," said Dunkum. "Give Jason a chance to catch up."

Jason Birchall ran along behind Eric.

Soon, Abby's brother Shawn came down Blossom Hill Lane. Like Jimmy, he was Korean. "I am very sorry to be late." It sounded like *velly* sorry.

"Nobody's late," Dunkum said, shooting one more basket.

But Dunkum's mom dashed across the lawn. "*I'm* late! I must enroll Ellen before she can attend school."

"Oops, I almost forgot," Dunkum said.

The girls covered their mouths, giggling.

"What's so funny?" Dunkum asked.

Abby swallowed another giggle. "Oh, nothing," she said.

Eric tossed the basketball to Jason.

Jason bounced the ball slowly. He stared at Ellen and Honey. "Who's the new girl?" he asked.

"Everybody, meet my cousin Ellen. Ellen, meet Eric Hagel, Shawn Hunter, and Jason Birchall." Dunkum sounded like he was making a speech.

"Now we *are* going to be late!" Eric complained.

The kids turned and hurried down the walk.

Jason watched Honey guide Ellen forward. "How will the dog know when to cross the street?" he asked.

"She's trained to listen for cars," Dunkum said. "Just watch when we get to the curb."

Abby's sister, Carly, suddenly dropped her show-and-tell. It was a giant green lizard puppet with a long tail.

Honey began barking loudly.

Ellen frowned and stopped walking. "What's wrong with Honey?" She tightened her hold on the harness.

"It's OK, Ellen," said Dunkum. "It's just Carly's ugly puppet."

"She's *not* ugly!" shouted Carly.

Dunkum chuckled. "It's a *she*?"

"God made girl lizards, too," Carly said, grinning.

"You're right," said Dunkum. "I forgot." He circled the girls, bouncing the ball.

The Cul-de-Sac Kids laughed as they reached the end of the block.

Honey led Ellen to the curb. They waited for a moment. A car passed by slowly, and Honey stepped back. Ellen did, too.

Soon, it was safe. The dog guided Ellen across the street to school.

"Wow," said Carly and Dee Dee.

"Honey's cool," said Eric.

Dunkum's mother took Ellen and her dog to the school office. The kids yelled their good-byes. They promised to meet at recess.

"Now two things will be exciting this week," Abby said. "One is School Spirit Day. The second thing is having a dog for a classmate."

"No kidding," said Stacy. Her eyes were bright.

Abby could hardly wait for school to start!

# Two

**M**iss Hershey was seating a girl with red pigtails.

"Looks like we have *another* new girl," Abby said. She tried not to stare.

Stacy opened her desk behind Abby's.

Abby watched her friend dig through her desk. "What are you looking for?" she asked.

"A piece of paper," Stacy muttered. She closed her desk quickly.

Abby ripped a page from her notebook. "Here." She gave the paper to Stacy.

Stacy began to draw a secret message for the new girl. The letters and numbers spelled out something special.

Well + come 2 R Class

"Will you take this to the new girl?" she asked.

"*You* take it. Don't be shy," Abby said. She pushed the note back into Stacy's hand.

Stacy wrinkled her face. Then she crept across the room. She slid the note onto the new girl's desk. Then she hurried back to her own desk.

Abby and Stacy watched the new girl open the note. She gave them a weird smile.

Stacy smiled back. Abby didn't know whether to smile or frown.

Jason plopped down on Abby's desk. "Hey, look at that. The new girl's got red pigtails."

"So what?" said Abby.

"Don't you see? Her hair's too short for pigtails," Jason joked. "They stick straight out."

"Be nice," Abby said. "She's new. Besides, we should treat others the way *we* want to be treated."

Jason crossed his eyes and scrunched up his face.

*Brr-i-i-ing!* The last bell before school started.

Miss Hershey's students scrambled to

their seats. She called roll. Then she asked the new girl to stand and say her name.

"I'm Leslie Groff," said the girl. She sat down real fast.

Abby thought Leslie must surely be in the wrong class. Leslie was way too short for their grade.

■■■

After spelling class, Ellen and her guide dog showed up.

Miss Hershey assigned a desk to Ellen in the back of the room. Honey could stretch out there.

Abby couldn't help staring at Honey. Her classmates kept looking at the beautiful dog, too.

"Students, please face the front," Miss Hershey said several times during math.

When it was time for reading, Leslie Groff sat beside Abby. Halfway through the story, she whispered, "I have a secret."

Abby looked at her. "A secret? What is it?"

"Can't tell," she whispered.

"Then let me guess," Abby said.

"You'll never guess in a trillion and one years."

A mystery! Abby was ready for the challenge. Her mind was racing. She *had* to solve it . . . whatever the mystery was!

At recess, Abby played with the other Cul-de-Sac Kids. They gathered near the slide beside Ellen and Honey. Abby asked, "What could Leslie's secret be?"

Dunkum had an idea. "Maybe she's a cousin to Anne of Green Gables. *She* had red hair, too."

They cracked up laughing.

"Leslie looks like a second grader to me. She probably skipped a grade," said Eric.

"I think so, too!" said Abby. "That's got to be her secret."

Ellen sat on the end of the slide. Honey was licking her hand. "Where's Leslie now?" Ellen asked.

"She stayed inside with Miss Hershey," Jason said. "Leslie's short, skinny pigtails match her legs!" He doubled over, laughing hard.

Abby didn't think it was funny. "Jason, what about the Golden Rule?"

"That's right," said Dunkum. "Besides, some kids can't help being skinny."

"And some kids can't help being *girls*!" joked Jason.

"Come on, Jason, let's play ball," Dunkum suggested. "The girls are gonna clobber you!"

Eric smiled at Abby. "Jason didn't really mean it, you know." He ran off to join the boys.

Ellen giggled. "Uh-oh, Abby. Eric *likes* you."

"Why do you think that?" asked Abby.

"I just do," said Ellen.

The recess bell rang.

On the way inside, Ellen promised to show Abby and Stacy her Braille machine. "It makes little dots stick up off paper. I can feel each dot with my fingers," Ellen explained. "That's how I read."

"It's like a secret code," Abby said. "Which reminds me of Leslie Groff. I *have* to figure out her secret!"

# Three

The next day, Abby's father woke her. "Hurry, Abby. You overslept!"

She sat up in bed and rubbed her eyes. "Wha-at?"

"Fifteen minutes before breakfast," her father said. "Quick, or you'll be late for school!"

Abby tossed off the covers. She threw on a top and pants. She swished a toothbrush over her teeth and brushed her hair. Grabbing *Mystery History*, she was off to breakfast.

But the kitchen was empty.

"Daddy?"

"I'm in here," he called from his study.

"Where *is* everybody?" she asked.

He looked at his watch. "Well, my goodness! It's only six o'clock."

"Daddy!" Abby squealed. "You tricked me."

He gave her a bear hug. "Happy School Spirit Day, honey."

"You're getting me ready for the fun at school, right?"

Her father winked, wearing a big smile.

Then Abby had an idea.

She tiptoed to her sister's room. "Ps-st, Carly!"

Carly rolled over in bed. She rubbed her eyes and stretched.

Abby tried to sound serious. "If you don't hurry, you'll be late for school."

Carly looked at her big sister, already dressed for school. She jumped out of bed, but her foot stuck in the covers. Carly rolled, falling to the floor. *Thud!*

"Here, I'll help you." Abby untangled the covers for Carly. She pulled her foot out, too, and made sure she was okay. All the while, she tried not to burst out laughing.

While her sister hurried to the bathroom, Abby hid behind the bedroom door. Soon she heard Carly rush off to the kitchen.

Things were very quiet. But only for a moment.

"Abby!" wailed Carly. "No one's up! What's going on?"

Abby inched out of hiding. "Happy School Spirit Day!" she said.

"But this isn't school," Carly said. "This is our home." She crawled back into her unmade bed. "You'll be sorry for this," she grumbled.

"Aw, don't be mad," said Abby. "Now you'll have time to make your bed and pick up your room *before* school starts."

"Hey, you're not the boss!" said Carly. She threw her pillow at Abby.

Abby ran to her own room and slammed the door. Carly chased her. She pounded on Abby's door.

"What's all the racket?" Mom called sleepily.

Abby tried not to giggle. She secretly blamed Carly for all the noise.

"Please tell your sister to be quieter," their mother said.

"I will," Abby called back with a grin.

■■■

At school, Miss Hershey was wearing a purple suit. Her jacket was on backward. Her earrings were clipped on backward, too. Even the day's schedule was written on the chalkboard backward.

Abby looked hard at the jumbled words. *Hooray!* Reading class was first.

"Happy School Spirit Day," Miss Hershey told the class. "For several months now, we've been reading mysteries. All of you are learning to gather clues." She made her voice sound a little sneaky. "So . . . pay very close attention. You never know where a mystery might pop up."

Abby wondered about Leslie Groff's secret. Before class, Leslie had dropped a note on Abby's desk. Abby pulled it out and read it again. It was in a code, with pictures and words mixed up.

"Class, we're having art first today," their teacher said.

Jason raised his hand. "I don't get it. The schedule says reading is first."

Miss Hershey nodded. "Just remember— anything can happen today." There was that mysterious sound in her voice again.

2 the girl who ♡s mysteries.

🔋 U guess M + 🐝 C + cret?

🐝 give U till the N + 2 of school 2t day.

6 hours, not counting lunch.

LG

Abby was all ears. She listened carefully when Miss Hershey assigned them to tables.

She hid her book under the table during art. She couldn't wait to read the last chapter of *Mystery History*.

Leslie sat on the other side of the table. "What are you doing?" she asked.

Abby held up the book. "I'm going to guess your secret today. *This* will help me."

"Do you really think so?" asked Leslie. She had a funny look in her eyes.

"Yep."

"How would you like one clue?" Leslie asked.

"Double dabble good!" said Abby. She was ready.

Leslie's smile was sneaky. "OK, here goes." She leaned closer.

Abby closed her book. She sat up straight.

"Remember, things aren't always as they seem," Leslie whispered.

*That's not a clue*, Abby thought. "Give me a better one," she said.

"My father is a king." Leslie's voice was sly. "How's that for a clue?"

"But is it true?" asked Abby.

"Maybe, maybe not," said Leslie.

Abby knew about presidents. But kings and queens? Who was this girl trying to fool?

■ ■ ■

After art, Miss Hershey announced a special reading assignment. "I'm handing out a test. You must complete it before math class."

Tests were icksville for Abby. She waved her pencil at Leslie Groff. Leslie smiled back. But it was another sneaky smile. *What could Leslie's secret be?* Abby wondered.

Miss Hershey gave directions. "Remember, read *all* the questions first."

Abby glanced back at Ellen. Honey was taking a nap at Ellen's feet. Abby got up to sharpen her pencil. She passed Ellen's desk on the way. She peeked at Ellen's test. *So this is Braille*, she thought.

The classroom was suddenly very quiet. Everyone was working hard on the tests.

Soon, Honey was guiding Ellen to Miss Hershey's desk.

*She can't be finished yet*, thought Abby. She looked at her own paper. She was only on number seven.

A few minutes later, Leslie Groff was finished. Then Dunkum and Stacy.

Abby looked around the room. She was getting worried. *Something's wrong*, she thought. *Very wrong!*

# Four

**A**bby noticed Jason still doing his test. *Good*, she thought, *I'm not the only one*.

Miss Hershey turned away from the chalkboard. "For students who are still working, remember to read *all* the questions first," she reminded them.

Abby put her pencil down and read each question. The last question was: *If you have read all the questions, please write only your name, address, and telephone number at the bottom of this page. Then turn in the test.*

*Very tricky*, Abby thought. *I didn't follow the directions.*

Quickly, she wrote her name, address, and

telephone number at the bottom of the page. Then she scooted down in her seat.

"What are you doing?" Stacy whispered behind Abby.

"I feel like crawling under my desk," she whispered back. "I'm so embarrassed."

Then Abby heard Miss Hershey's voice. "Will you please give Jason a hint about the test, Abby?"

Her mouth was as dry as if she'd eaten chalk. Dry and yucky.

She looked at Jason. *Poor Jason. He's still working.*

Abby's voice cracked as she said, "Don't write anything until you read the whole page."

Jason twirled his pencil. He read to the bottom of the test. Suddenly, his face turned Christmas red. "Oh, *now* I get it," he said. "Good trick, Miss Hershey."

The class howled with laughter, including Jason.

What a double dabble good joke!

Miss Hershey glanced around the room. "Now, listen very carefully. Following directions is a good thing to do every day. Not only

School Spirit Day." With that, the teacher winked at Leslie.

Abby blinked. She turned around. "Did you see that?" she asked Stacy.

Stacy nodded. "Something's up."

"OK, it's time for some riddle fun," said Miss Hershey. "Anyone?"

Dunkum raised his hand. "*I've* got a riddle. What do you get when you cross a duck with a cow?"

"Anyone know?" Miss Hershey asked, looking around.

No one answered.

"Quackers and milk!" said Dunkum with glee.

Everyone clapped.

"Yay, Dunkum!" shouted Jason.

"Go, Dunkum!" said Eric more softly.

Ellen raised her hand next.

"Yes?" Miss Hershey said.

Ellen smiled so big, her face seemed to light up. "What is the beginning of eternity, the end of time and space, the beginning of every end, and the end of every race?" she asked.

Stacy whispered, "What a mouthful."

Miss Hershey nodded. "That's an excellent question, Ellen. Does anyone know the answer?"

The students looked puzzled.

At last, Jason raised his hand.

"Go ahead, Jason," Miss Hershey said.

He grinned and shook his head. "Sorry," he said. "I don't know the answer. I can't even figure out the question!"

The kids were laughing again.

Miss Hershey looked at Ellen. "I believe you've stumped us. Please tell us the answer."

"The answer is the letter E," Ellen replied.

The kids clapped for Ellen's riddle. Abby clapped extra hard.

Jason raised his hand again. He still looked confused. "I don't get it," he admitted.

Leslie giggled.

Miss Hershey explained. "E begins the words *eternity* and *end*. And E ends the words *time, space*, and *race*."

Jason was nodding at his desk. "Oh yeah!" he said. "Very cool."

Leslie raised her hand. "*I* have a riddle, too."

"Yes, Leslie?" Miss Hershey said.

"If all of you lived to be a trillion and one years old, you could never guess my secret."

*Never?* Abby held her breath.

She thought about Leslie's first clue, earlier today. Many kings and queens lived in England, long ago. Maybe that *was* a good clue, after all. Abby waved her hand high. "Are you from England, and did you skip second grade?" she asked.

"Nope to both guesses," Leslie said. Her grin turned from sneaky to unkind.

Time was ticking away. Abby had less than six hours left at school today. And she didn't like it. Not one bit.

# Five

Time for lunch.

Abby slipped into line with Stacy. Jason cut in line behind her. Leslie squealed.

In a flash, Miss Hershey pulled Jason out of line. The rest of the class headed off to lunch.

The older Cul-de-Sac Kids always ate together at school. Today, Jason came in five minutes late. He plodded across the floor to their table. "I got in trouble," he explained. "And all because Leslie Groff screamed!"

Jason scooted into the seat and opened his lunch. He poked his nose inside, then slammed the sack shut. "Anybody want to trade?" he pleaded.

"What's in there?" Dunkum asked.

"Rabbit food," Jason replied. He pulled a face.

Dunkum held out his hand for Jason's carrot and celery sticks. "I'll trade your veggies for my orange pieces."

"It's a deal," Jason said.

Next thing, all the kids started trading food. Eric even gave away his chocolate-chip cookie. To Abby.

Abby was double dabble glad about that. "Thanks, Eric." She wondered if Ellen was right about Eric. Maybe he *did* like her extra-special.

Well, Abby liked him, too. They went to the same church and both liked mystery books. Besides that, Eric's mom made great chocolate-chip cookies. "Yum," she said, enjoying every bite.

■■■

The kids chattered off and on about Leslie.

"Any ideas about her secret?" Eric asked Abby.

Abby shook her head. "Not yet."

"I think Leslie *looks* like a second grader," Stacy said. "But nothing like a princess."

"She doesn't act like royalty," Jason said. He was being more serious now.

Abby scratched her head. "So . . . what could the secret be?"

"Maybe she has a twin sister," suggested Jason. "And her twin got all the hair."

The kids laughed. A piece of Dunkum's sandwich flew out of his mouth.

The kids cackled some more.

"Maybe she's a friend of Miss Hershey," said Stacy.

"Or a neighbor," said Shawn.

"Could Leslie be Miss Hershey's relative?" Jason asked.

"I saw Miss Hershey wink at Leslie. Abby saw it, too," Stacy said.

Abby nodded. "There's something really weird going on."

"Leslie doesn't look like Miss Hershey at all," said Dunkum.

"Yeah, and Miss Hershey isn't a queen," said Jason. "And her husband can't be a king—"

"Because Miss Hershey isn't married!" Abby broke in.

"Hey . . . maybe the king rules on a secret island somewhere," said Eric.

"Yeah, *right*," Abby replied. "This is getting us nowhere. We need solid clues."

Ellen had an idea. "Maybe there isn't any secret. Maybe *that's* the secret."

Jason sputtered between apple bites. "Leslie better not set us up for nothing."

"Jason's right," Abby said. "That would be a mean trick."

Just then, Leslie approached their table. She was licking a pink lollipop. "What's Jason right about?" She glared at him.

The Cul-de-Sac Kids were silent.

# Six

Leslie repeated her question. "Are you going to tell me or not? What's Jason right about?"

Jason ignored her. He slurped on his apple and spit out the seeds. Then he stuffed them into his shirt pocket.

Abby giggled about the seeds.

Without blinking, he said, "You never know when I might get hungry."

The kids roared with laughter.

Leslie's face turned red. "You're a big show-off!"

"*You* can't call him that," Dunkum scolded.

"And why not?" Leslie demanded, her hands on her hips.

Dunkum scowled at Leslie.

She began to squirm and opened her mouth to say something. But the lunchroom teacher marched over to their table. All of them were sent out for recess.

But Leslie didn't head for the playground. She walked back toward the classroom.

*Where's she going?* Abby wondered. She wanted to follow Leslie, but her friends called to her from the doorway.

"OK, I'm coming!" Abby said.

■■■

Outside, Abby and Stacy hung upside down from the monkey bars. Ellen's guide dog, Honey, rested in the sand nearby.

Abby kept her eyes on Ellen, who was swinging straight across the bars. "You're good at that," she said.

"Thanks," Ellen replied.

"I've never known a blind person before," Stacy said. "I wondered what you were like."

Ellen swung on the bars. "I'm no different than anybody else."

Abby thought about that. "Your riddle was terrific," she said. "Did you make it up?"

Ellen dropped down from the bars. "I listen

to the radio and TV a lot. If I hear something once, I never forget it."

"That's so cool," Stacy whispered.

"Can you keep a secret?" Abby asked.

"Sure," both girls answered.

"I'm going to play a joke on Miss Hershey."

"You are?" Stacy whispered. She moved closer to Abby. "Tell us more."

"I'm going to make the whole class disappear."

Ellen coughed. "How?"

"During library, when Miss Hershey has a break, I'll ask the librarian to tell the class about it. Then, during social studies, I'll see if the principal will page Miss Hershey. When she gets back from the office—*poof!* The whole class just disappeared to the library!"

"Will the principal and librarian help you?" asked Ellen.

"I think so," Abby said. "Mr. Romerez, the librarian, is a friend of my dad. And Mrs. Millar teaches Sunday school at our church. She likes a good practical joke. I'm sure she'll help me play a trick on Miss Hershey."

"Your plan sounds great," said Ellen. "I hope it works."

"Too bad we won't get to see Miss Hershey's face!" Stacy said.

When the kids filed in from recess, Leslie was sliding her desk close to the teacher's.

*Now what's she doing?* Abby wondered. She picked up her pencil and headed for the pencil sharpener.

When she walked past Ellen's desk, Ellen touched her arm. "Abby, please bring Leslie here to me," she said.

Abby was startled. "How did you know it was me?"

"Oh, by the way you smell," Ellen said, a big smile on her face. "And . . . that's a *good* thing."

*Amazing!* thought Abby. She hurried to get Leslie before the bell rang. And before time for library.

"Hey, Leslie," said Ellen. She stretched her hand out. "I didn't meet you yesterday. I'm Ellen Mifflin. I guess we should stick together, since we're the new girls, right?"

Leslie was silent at first. Then she said, "But we don't *have* to, do we?"

Abby studied Leslie. *God's Word teaches us to love each other, but some people are harder to love. Leslie Groff is one of them. What* is *her problem? And what is her secret?*

Ellen didn't seem to mind Leslie's rudeness. "Maybe we could play together at recess," she suggested.

"Maybe," Leslie replied. She tapped Ellen's hand. "There, I gave you five."

*Will Leslie really go outside for the last recess?* Abby wondered. *Why did she stay inside, anyway? Is she allergic to the sun or something?* Abby had read about kids like that. But no, that couldn't be Leslie's secret.

*What about her crazy story? Is her father* really *a king?* Abby doubted it. Leslie didn't act very much like a princess.

*The whole thing must be a lie,* Abby decided. She would watch Leslie even more closely. Every move and every word.

Like a good detective.

# Seven

In the library, Abby whispered her secret plan. Both the librarian and the principal agreed to help the class disappear. Just as she hoped!

Abby would hide in the closet while the class tiptoed to the library. She couldn't wait to see Miss Hershey's face.

So, the secret was set.

■ ■ ■

During social studies, Mrs. Millar, the principal, called Miss Hershey over the intercom. "Please come to the office, Miss Hershey," the principal said.

"I'll be right there," Miss Hershey replied. She told the class to keep busy. "No visiting with friends," she said. Then she left for the office. "I'll return in a minute."

The second she was gone, the entire class tiptoed to the library.

All but Abby. She sneaked to the closet and left the door open just a crack. Perfect!

Soon Miss Hershey returned. "Oh my!" she gasped. "Where is my class?"

Abby giggled silently in the closet.

The trick had worked! The teacher *was* surprised. School Spirit Day was so much fun.

While Abby was still hiding, Miss Hershey did a strange thing. She went to Leslie's desk and opened it. Out came a red coin purse. Miss Hershey slipped her hand into the pocket of her backward suit jacket.

Abby watched closely. She saw Miss Hershey put some money in Leslie's purse!

Abby leaped out of the closet. "Surprise!"

"My goodness—Abby!" Miss Hershey said, startled. "Where *is* everyone?"

"They disappeared," shouted Abby. She clapped her hands. "It worked. We really fooled you."

"You certainly did," Miss Hershey said. "Where are they *really*?"

"In the library," Abby told her.

"Will you tell them to return to class now?" Miss Hershey asked.

Abby was eager to ask about the money. And the red coin purse. "Do you know Leslie's secret?" she asked.

Miss Hershey nodded. "Yes."

"Will she tell us today?" Abby asked.

"I think Leslie hopes someone will *guess* her secret," said Miss Hershey, smiling.

"This is turning into a real mystery," Abby said.

But Miss Hershey said no more.

Abby scratched her head. What was going on?

She hurried to the office. The principal let her talk over the intercom. "Operation Disappearing Class is a success. Miss Hershey's students, please return to your classroom."

Mrs. Millar patted Abby's shoulder. "School Spirit Day comes just once a year. Back to work now."

But it was already time for afternoon recess.

Miss Hershey's classroom door swung wide. Kids dashed out to the playground.

Leslie ran outside, too.

"Will we find out your secret today?" Abby asked her.

Leslie ran to the swings. She shouted over her shoulder, "Someone has to guess it first! And you don't have much time left."

Leslie's answer bugged Abby. She wanted to know the secret *now*!

Ellen was playing on the monkey bars. Her guide dog waited in the sand below. While Leslie was swinging, Ellen said, "I think I know Leslie's secret."

Abby stared at her. "You do?"

"Give us a clue, OK?" Stacy begged.

"Just keep your eyes on Leslie," Ellen said. "That's all I'm saying."

"But we *are* watching," Stacy insisted. "All the time!"

"Yeah," Abby said. "I'm tired of watching her." She wondered about Miss Hershey's actions while Abby was hiding in the closet.

"How do you know Leslie's secret?" asked Stacy.

Ellen laughed. "I guess my insight comes in handy sometimes."

They ran to the swings and played.

Then Ellen had an idea. "Let's play Twenty Questions with Leslie," she said.

"Double dabble good idea!" exclaimed Abby. "Maybe we'll get some more clues!" She turned toward Leslie's swing.

But Leslie had vanished!

"Leslie disappeared," said Abby, looking all around.

"Hey, look over there," said Stacy. "I see her."

"Leslie's running races with the boys," said Abby.

"Come on," Ellen said. "Honey needs to walk."

"OK," Abby said.

Dunkum and Eric were squatting in their get-set-go positions.

Jason yelled, "Are you ready?"

The boys shouted they were.

Abby could hardly keep her own secret inside. She had to tell Stacy and Ellen. "I saw something while I was hiding."

"Something in the closet?" Ellen asked.

"No, something *outside* the closet. Just listen to this: Miss Hershey put some money in Leslie's coin purse."

"What?" Stacy said.

"When I hid in the closet, I saw Miss Hershey open Leslie's desk," Abby explained.

"That's weird," Stacy said.

"What was Miss Hershey doing in the new girl's purse?" Ellen asked.

"How should I know?" Abby said. "It's very strange."

The girls watched the races. Soon, Abby's eyes grew wide. Leslie was ahead of the boys! Abby described the entire scene to Ellen.

"Well, that fits," Ellen said softly. "Leslie really likes to show off."

Abby wished she knew *everything* Ellen knew about Leslie. She closed her eyes and pretended to be blind.

She listened. The sounds seemed sharper all around her.

She sniffed. The smells seemed stronger, too.

Suddenly, she heard yelling. She opened

her eyes. It was Jason. He was chasing Leslie across the soccer field.

Abby blinked twice. She'd never seen him run so fast.

What was happening?

# Eight

Abby stared across the playground. *This is crazy*, she thought.

Jason was running after Leslie! He was huffing and puffing. His hair was flying with every bounce.

But Leslie was far ahead of him.

Abby shouted, "Look at Jason go!"

*Br-r-ring!* The recess bell rang.

Jason chased Leslie around the playground and back to the school door. She raced through the door, past kids in line.

"I'm going to get that girl," Jason hollered, wiping his face.

"What did she do?" Abby asked.

"She called me a show-off again," he bellowed. "She's got no right."

Later, in the girls' bathroom, Leslie complained about Jason. "He's so hyper. Never sits still," she told Stacy and Abby.

"Oh, that's just Jason," Abby said.

Leslie pulled hard on her stubby pigtails. "How can you *say* that? He's disgusting!"

"Jason's our friend," Stacy spoke up.

"Yeah, and it doesn't make any difference to us if he's hyper."

Stacy stepped forward. "It's what's inside that counts, Leslie!" she said.

Leslie's mouth dropped open. "I thought you were *shy*." She popped some candy in her mouth and left.

"Way to go, Stacy!" Abby said. "I didn't think you'd ever talk to her like that!"

Stacy blushed. "I hope she's not mad. I didn't want to be mean."

"You were just telling the truth," Abby said. "And I don't think you can be mean. You're the nicest person I know!"

Stacy's face grew red again. "I try to live the way God wants me to."

"It would be nice if everybody did that," said Abby.

Back in the room, Stacy and Abby took

their seats. Miss Hershey asked the class to write their numbers. "To 300," she said.

Abby gulped. *We won't get done before the end of the day*, she thought. *And I still haven't figured out Leslie's secret.*

She started writing. 1, 2, 3, 4 . . .

Abby looked at Leslie. 23, 24, 25 . . .

Dunkum sneezed. 48, 49, 50 . . .

Eric dropped his pencil. 76, 77, 78 . . .

Abby was up to 153 when Miss Hershey announced, "OK, class. Stop writing. How many of you wrote two, three, zero, zero?" She wrote the number on the board.

Dunkum said, "We weren't supposed to write the numbers *up to* 300. You wanted us to write 2 . . . 3 . . . 0 . . . 0. Two thousand three hundred."

Abby groaned. Miss Hershey had tricked them again!

"You keep fooling us," said Jason.

"What fun," said Leslie.

Abby looked at the clock. Almost time to go home. She wasn't even close to figuring out Leslie's secret.

Abby raised her hand. "May we play

Twenty Questions until we guess Leslie's secret?"

Miss Hershey turned to Leslie, who hopped up to the front of the room.

"Who's first?" Leslie asked.

Four hands popped up.

Dunkum asked, "Are you an alien?"

"Good guess," whispered Abby.

Leslie laughed. She shook her head. Her stubby pigtails poked out farther than ever.

Jason was next. "Are you a twin?"

Abby held her breath. Whew! Jason didn't say anything about the other twin with all the hair.

"No way," said Leslie.

Eric's hand was high. "Do you sing in the shower with a British accent?"

The kids laughed. So did Leslie.

*That* wasn't it.

Abby's turn. "Did Miss Hershey owe you some money?"

Leslie looked puzzled. She turned to the teacher. "How did she know?"

Abby waited. She felt like a detective close to cracking a case.

Leslie nodded. "Miss Hershey owed me some money."

"Why?" Abby asked.

"We made a deal. If the class guessed my secret before lunch, I owed her a dollar. But if no one guessed by then, she owed me," Leslie explained.

*Why would the teacher make a deal like that?* thought Abby.

Abby studied the new girl.

Leslie's eyes danced. She was having too much fun with this secret. Maybe she didn't want the mystery to be solved at all.

Suddenly, Honey barked loudly. She was straining on her harness. She seemed to be pulling Ellen away from the desk.

"What's wrong with Honey?" Abby asked.

Honey sniffed the air. *Woof!* She began to bark.

Then Ellen shouted, "Miss Hershey, I smell smoke!"

At that moment, the fire alarm sounded.

# Nine

"Students, please line up quickly!" Miss Hershey said. The fire alarm kept ringing.

Abby was nervous. She got in line behind Ellen and her dog. Dunkum held the door.

Miss Hershey grabbed Leslie's hand as they left the classroom. She was still holding it when the line formed away from the building.

Abby watched closely. *Why would Miss Hershey hold Leslie's hand?*

"Is the school on fire?" yelled Jason.

Ellen held on to Honey's harness. "I hope not," she said.

"Just think, if the alarm hadn't sounded, Honey might have saved our lives," said Eric.

"Because Honey smelled the smoke!" said Abby.

"Wow," said Stacy. "I'm impressed."

In the front of the line, Leslie stared back at them.

But Abby smiled at her. "Leslie's watching us," she whispered to Ellen, who was petting her dog.

"I definitely know her secret," Ellen said slowly. "But first, I have a riddle for *her*."

Miss Hershey left the line to talk to another teacher.

"Get Leslie into line with us," Abby whispered.

"OK," Dunkum said. "I'll get her."

Soon, Leslie came running over.

"Ellen says she knows your secret," Abby declared.

Leslie put her hands on her hips. "Really?"

Ellen coughed. "Who is the mother of Jesus?"

Leslie looked puzzled. "Everybody knows that. What does Mary in the Bible have to do with my secret?"

"Who was Mary in the Christmas play at Grace Church two years ago?"

Leslie's face went white. "How should I know?" she stuttered.

"Because *you* were Mary in the Christmas play," said Ellen.

"How do you know that?" Leslie asked.

"I have a good memory," Ellen replied.

"But you didn't see me, did you?" said Leslie.

"No, but I heard you say your lines," said Ellen. "So did my cousin, Dunkum."

"Really?" Leslie asked. "You remember my voice?"

"I sure do," Ellen said.

Abby could not picture the mother of Jesus with stubby pigtails.

"You're right," said Leslie. "I was Mary. But that's not my secret. What else do you know about me?"

Ellen said, "Well, you had a different last name then."

Abby started adding up the clues. She checked them off in her head.

1. Miss Hershey winked at Leslie.

2. Leslie stayed inside with Miss Hershey during recess.

3. She moved her desk close to Miss Hershey's.

4. Miss Hershey knew Leslie's secret.

5. Miss Hershey owed Leslie money. She knew where Leslie's coin purse was.

6. Miss Hershey grabbed Leslie's hand during the fire alarm.

Abby thought it over like a good detective. She scratched her head. The clues all led to one person—their teacher.

"I've got it!" Abby shouted. "You're Miss Hershey's niece or cousin or something!"

Eric said, "No way! Leslie doesn't look anything like Miss Hershey."

"Maybe she's adopted," Stacy suggested.

Leslie looked surprised. "That's it! All of you are right."

"We are?" said Stacy, grinning.

There were some unanswered questions. Like any super sleuth, Abby refused to leave any loose ends.

"Why is your last name Groff and not Hershey?" Abby asked.

"I made up the name Groff," Leslie said, giggling. "Just for today."

"What about your father? Is he really a king?" Abby demanded.

"Oh, that," said Leslie. "I wanted to lead you astray."

"I knew it!" Abby said. "You tricked us on purpose."

Eric objected. "But that wasn't a fair clue."

"Clues are clues," said Leslie. "Some lead you off the track."

Abby wished Leslie had been nicer about the whole thing.

"Why doesn't Dunkum remember Leslie?" Abby asked Ellen.

"Well, he should have . . . because *he* was Joseph!" Ellen laughed. "I told you Dunkum is forgetful!"

Abby and Stacy laughed. Dunkum didn't seem to mind. He leaped up and pretended to shoot a basket.

Jason wasn't laughing. He was staring at Leslie. He was frowning hard.

Just then, two fire trucks roared up.

"They're too late," said Dunkum. "Look!"

Coming out the back door, the principal carried a fire extinguisher. She held it high over her head.

The kids' cheering echoed around the playground.

Soon the all-clear bell sounded. The kids filed inside.

Outside the classroom door, Jason pulled Abby aside. "You've got to help me," he whispered.

Jason's face was as white as a sheet!

# Ten

**W**hat's wrong with you, Jason?" Abby asked.

"Leslie's mad at me. That's what." Jason stopped. "And I've been mean to her. And . . ."

Abby looked at her watch. "And there's not much time left of school today. What can you do to patch things up?" she asked.

"Think of something, will you?" Jason pleaded.

"I'll try." Abby couldn't think of much.

The kids took their seats, and Leslie whispered something to Miss Hershey.

Miss Hershey looked surprised. Then she put her hands on Leslie's shoulders. "Class, I am happy to introduce my niece to you.

Her name is Leslie *Hershey*. She tells me you are all very good detectives."

The kids cheered. "Yahoo!"

Jason put his head down.

"What clues helped you most?" their teacher asked.

Abby raised her hand. "When you grabbed Leslie's hand during the fire alarm. That's something an aunt would probably do."

Stacy shot her hand up. "Leslie didn't come out for recess. If my aunt was the teacher, I might stay in and help her, too."

"Yeah, and she moved her desk next to yours," added Eric.

"But she doesn't look like you, Miss Hershey," said Dunkum. "That was real tricky!"

Miss Hershey smiled. "Leslie has been out of school for teacher work days. I wanted her to visit my class. But it was Leslie's idea to keep her identity a secret. Was it good practice for solving mysteries?"

"Yes!" cried the class. Everyone clapped. Except Jason.

"Can we solve another mystery sometime?" Abby asked. She *loved* mysteries.

"That's a good idea. But now it's time to announce this week's student of the week."

Miss Hershey took a large candy bar from her desk drawer. The student of the week would be eating it soon! "Jason Birchall, you're the student of the week."

Jason sat up tall at his desk. "Thanks, Miss Hershey." He took the candy bar and popped it into his shirt pocket.

Miss Hershey reminded him to bring baby pictures and family pictures for the bulletin board. And a list of his favorite things: books, games, and people.

Jason's favorite thing to do was *not* a secret. He liked to pig out on food. Mostly junk food.

Suddenly, Abby knew how to help Jason settle things with Leslie. But did she have time to tell him before the bell rang?

Quickly, she printed a note. Jason must *not* eat the candy bar in his pocket!

Jason scrunched his face into a frown when he read the note. He stared at Abby. "Why not?" he mouthed.

"Trust me," she mouthed back.

*Brr-i-i-ing!* The final bell.

298

Miss Hershey made an announcement. "Leslie will return to her own school tomorrow," she said. "Maybe she can come back for another visit sometime."

The kids called good-bye to Leslie.

Abby rushed to Jason's desk. "Hurry or you'll be too late." She glanced at Leslie. She was cleaning out her desk.

"What should I do?" Jason whined.

Abby tapped on the candy bar through his shirt pocket. The apple seeds were still in there, too. "Here's your answer," she said. "If you want to win her over, give her your candy bar."

Jason sighed. "How do you know it'll work?"

"Remember the Golden Rule? Treat others the way you want to be treated. Leslie *loves* sweets."

"That makes two of us." Slowly, he pulled the candy bar out of its hiding place. He held it in his hand. "I shouldn't eat this," he said sadly. "It cancels out the good stuff I had for lunch."

He held the candy bar to his nose. He breathed deeply. "Smells great," he said with glazed eyes. Then he saw the teacher's niece packing her things.

"Better decide now," Abby said. "She's on her way home."

Leslie and Miss Hershey walked out the door and into the hallway.

"Leslie, wait!" Jason called.

Leslie stopped. She looked surprised. Turning to her aunt, she said, "Go ahead. I'll catch up in a second."

Abby watched from the door. She heard Jason say he was sorry about chasing Leslie. Then he offered her the candy bar.

Abby held her breath. *Please be nice, Leslie.*

Leslie raised her eyebrows. She looked embarrassed. "Thanks," Leslie said quietly. "You're A-OK!"

Jason took a deep breath. "You're OK, too." He paused.

*Now what?* thought Abby.

"Uh, you can call me a show-off if you want to."

"So . . . we're friends?" Leslie asked, smiling.

"Friends," he said.

Then Leslie unwrapped the candy bar and gave him half. "Show-off isn't the best name

for you," Leslie said. She pulled on her pigtails. "Sharer is much better."

Jason turned bright red.

Abby wished she had a camera. This was a perfect picture for the student of the week bulletin board. She hurried off to tell Stacy.

"Hey, Abby, wait up!" Jason called to her.

Abby laughed. She pretended to take his picture.

"Don't be silly." Jason held out his half of the candy bar. "Want a bite?"

Abby reached for it.

"Happy School Spirit Day!" he shouted, taking it back. In one bite, it was gone.

Abby wasn't finished with Jason. She had a great idea. "Race you home."

"I'm too tired," Jason said, munching.

"I have a feeling my mom made brownies," she said, starting to run.

Jason's eyes grew wide. He rubbed his stomach. He took off after Abby.

Abby raced across the playground to Blossom Hill Lane.

The other Cul-de-Sac Kids cheered as Jason ran all the way to Abby's porch. He collapsed on the steps. "OK, now let's have those brownies!"

"Just kidding," Abby shouted. "Happy School Spirit Day!"

Jason burst into laughter.

Abby wished School Spirit Day were closer than a whole year away.

# BOOK 24

# The Midnight Mystery

For
Kayla Erickson,
who loves to read.
And
for Erin Meyer,
who loves to write.

# One

The end of the school year had come at last!

Dunkum Mifflin had been counting the days. He was rip-roaring ready for summer.

He and Abby Hunter stood tall on the school stage. Miss Hershey's class was taking their curtain call. They bowed low as the audience clapped.

*Yahoo! End of school*, thought Dunkum.

The audience kept clapping.

Then . . . *swoosh!* The stage curtains dropped, and the lights went up. The Blossom Hill School spring play was finished. A smashing success.

Dunkum and Abby hurried backstage. The other Cul-de-Sac Kids were waiting in the

wings, behind the curtains. They were all smiles.

Abby was the president of the block club. Five boys and four girls. They loved adventure and solving mysteries. Their club slogan was "the Cul-de-Sac Kids stick together."

Dunkum removed his space-captain suit. Carefully, he placed it in the prop box. "What a cool play," he said.

Abby's eyes danced. "Lots better than last year!"

"Yep, sure was," Jason Birchall said. He was prancing and jiving about, as usual.

Eric Hagel and Jason gave Dunkum and Abby high fives. "All the practicing paid off," said Eric.

"Time to celebrate!" said Jason.

"Everyone's coming to my house," Dunkum said, grinning. He had sent out invitations for an ice-cream party.

Jason's eyes grew bigger. "What are we waiting for?" he asked. "Let's get going."

Eric and Stacy Henry agreed. "Junk food, here we come," Stacy said. And Eric gave a thumbs-up.

"We won't be in Miss Hershey's class next

year," Jason said. He tossed his space costume into the prop box.

"Don't worry about that now," Dunkum said. "Summer's finally here!"

Dunkum's blind cousin, Ellen Mifflin, came around the curtains. Honey, her guide dog, led the way. The dog wore a shiny blue space suit and black wire antennas. He had played a poochy part in the play—Space Dog.

Abby and her younger sister, Carly, and Carly's best friend, Dee Dee Winters, crowded around Space Dog. "So . . . how does Honey like show business?" asked Abby.

Ellen's eyes were closed. "Oh, she loves it. Don't you, girl?" She knelt down and hugged her dog. Ellen's long brown hair covered Honey's face.

"Wait till you see her brand-new tricks," Dunkum said. He took off the dog's costume and antennas.

"You're kidding. New tricks?" Abby asked. She sat beside Stacy, near Honey. The boys crowded around, too.

Ellen stood up, smiling. "Honey loves to perform. Don't you, big girl?"

*Woof, woof!* barked Honey.

"Give us a sneak preview," Eric pleaded.

A mischievous grin swept across Ellen's face. "Wait for the party," she said.

"Aw, why not now?" Jason begged.

"Because I need ice cream for the trick," Ellen said. She pushed her hair behind her ear.

"That reminds me," Dunkum said, looking at Jason. "Are you hungry for chocolate ice cream?"

Jason licked his lips and rubbed his stomach. "Wild pit bulls couldn't keep me away."

"Don't you mean wild *horses*?" Dunkum said.

"Horses, pit bulls . . . whatever." Jason pranced around.

"I know a good pit bull joke," Ellen said. She held on to her dog's harness. "Want to hear it?"

Honey barked and shook her head.

"Hey, it looks like Honey just said no." Jason and the other Cul-de-Sac Kids watched Ellen's guide dog closely.

"Better cover Honey's ears when you talk about pit bulls," Dunkum joked.

Ellen giggled and felt for Honey's ears.

"There," she said, finding them. "Now, what did the pit bull say when he sat on a pile of sandpaper?"

The kids looked at one another. They shrugged their shoulders.

"I think we give up," Dunkum said, eager to know. "What *did* the pit bull say when he sat on the sandpaper?"

Ellen's eyes were open, but they stared straight ahead. "Rough, rough." She giggled.

"Hey, that's a good joke," Jason said as he headed for the door. He was usually the last person to arrive anywhere. But when it came to sweets, Jason Birchall was first in line!

Dunkum's parents waved from the back of the room. "We'll see you at the party," Dunkum's dad called.

Dunkum's house was across the street from the school. He and his friends were going to walk to the party.

Abby and Stacy followed Ellen and her guide dog down the stage steps. Jason and Eric joined the girls near the outside door. So did Dunkum.

Adam Henny showed up just then. "Where's everyone going?" he asked.

"No place special," Dunkum lied.

Adam was the last person Dunkum wanted hanging around. Adam's clothes looked like toxic waste dump specials. Especially the ratty red T-shirt he had on today.

Besides that, Adam Henny was *not* a Cul-de-Sac Kid. No way was Dunkum going to invite an outsider to his party!

# TWO

Dunkum couldn't wait to leave. "Have a nice summer," he said to Adam.

The boy smiled a faint smile. He pushed his hand into his pants pocket and pulled out something. "Here's my phone number."

Dunkum shook his head. "Uh, no, that's OK," he said and rushed out the door. He wanted to forget about Adam. No sense messing up the end-of-school party over *that* kid.

His friends were waiting at the flagpole. "What kind of ice-cream toppings are we having?" asked Jason.

"That's not polite," Eric piped up. "Just wait and see."

Dunkum elbowed Eric's ribs. "Hey, relax,

Eric. School's out. It's pig-out time!" He began to name off all the toppings. "Jelly beans, chocolate sprinkles, strawberry syrup . . ." He paused. "Uh, I forgot the rest."

"Come on, try!" Jason pleaded.

"Dunkum's always forgetting stuff," Ellen said.

"It's a good thing Abby's our club president," Dunkum said. "*She* never forgets anything."

"And don't you forget it," Abby agreed.

It was true. Dunkum was a good detective only because Abby and the others were his partners. She paid attention to details. So far they'd solved every mystery known to man. Well . . . at least the ones on Blossom Hill Lane.

Dunkum waited at the curb for Honey to step into the street. Ellen gripped the harness with her left hand. "Honey, forward," she said.

But Honey waited for two more cars. When it was safe, she led Ellen across. "Good girl," Ellen said.

A black Jeep was parked in the driveway

across the street. On the back was a bumper sticker. It read *I ♥ pets!* A balding man was holding a fluffy gray cat.

"Hey, that's Mister Whiskers!" Dee Dee said, racing across the street.

"What's that man doing with your cat?" Dunkum asked, staring.

The man turned and frowned. "Poor thing. I found him just wandering around," he explained. He gave Dee Dee her cat.

"That's strange," Abby said. "I thought he stayed in the house."

"Mister Whiskers?" The man looked at the cat in Dee Dee's arms. "What a nice name." He stroked the cat.

"Mister Whiskers is a cool cul-de-sac cat," Jason said, nodding his head.

The man turned and looked at Honey. "That's one nice dog you've got there," he said.

"Thanks," Ellen said. "She's my eyes."

"I can see that," the man said. Suddenly, he got into his car.

"Thanks for taking care of my cat," Dee Dee called to him.

"Anytime," the man said out his car window.

The kids raced to Dunkum's house.

Party time!

■■■

In the kitchen, a row of ice-cream toppings lined the table.

Jason was the first to be served. "Hey, look!" he said. "There's a worm in my ice cream." He held up something green and wiggly. He waved it at Carly Hunter.

"Eew!" squealed Carly as Jason dropped the green gummy worm into his mouth.

Dunkum and Eric ate two worms each just plain.

Abby, Stacy, and Carly asked for waffle cones. Dunkum's father scooped up chocolate ice cream for them. He pushed the ice cream into their cones. "Some worms for the ladies?" he asked, smiling.

"Not for me, thanks," Stacy replied.

"How about sprinkles?" Dunkum's dad asked.

The girls nodded. "Sprinkles are fine, thanks," Abby said.

"They're really chocolate-covered ants, you know. Fried and dried," Dunkum teased.

"Double dabble yuck," Abby said, giggling. She slid in beside Ellen at the table.

Honey lay close to Ellen's feet, taking a snooze. The dog seemed at home in Dunkum's house. Ellen did, too.

Ellen's dad was out of the country with an overseas job. Dunkum didn't mind at all. It was lots of fun having Ellen and Honey visit for a couple months.

Dunkum's mom dished up some ice cream for Ellen. Honey's nose twitched, and she opened one eye. "I think it's time for Honey's performance," Dunkum said.

Eric sat across the table. He wiped off his chocolate mustache with a napkin. "Go for it."

Ellen reached down and touched her dog's head. "Honey, let's play Lickety-split."

Dunkum made a drum roll on the table.

All the kids watched closely.

Honey stood up. The tips of her ears stood

at attention. She kept her eyes on Ellen. Only Ellen.

"Hey, check it out. The dog obeys better than I do," Jason said, laughing.

"Honey is real smart," Dunkum said. "Just watch."

# Three

Dunkum scooped up some ice cream. He put it in a cone for Ellen. "One vanilla cone coming up," he said.

*Woof, woof!* Honey barked.

Ellen smiled. "You like this trick, don't you, girl?"

Honey barked again.

Dunkum handed the cone to Ellen. She held it in front of her and gave the command. "Honey, take two licks. But only two."

Honey's tongue slurped the cone. Twice.

All the kids clapped.

"That's double dabble amazing!" Abby said. "Our dog would *never* do that."

"Nope," little Carly said. "Our dog would bite the cone right out of your hand!"

"Wait . . . there's more," Ellen said softly.

Honey waited. Ears perked, tongue out.

Ellen gave the command. "Honey, take three licks."

The kids counted, "1 . . . 2 . . . 3," as Honey licked the cone.

Eric slapped his forehead. "I don't believe this!"

"I not, either," said Shawn, Abby's Korean brother.

"Tell Honey to take twenty licks," Jason shouted.

"She doesn't know *that* number," Ellen said. "But she knows *this*." Ellen held up the cone again.

Honey looked up at the ice cream.

"Honey," Ellen whispered. "Lickety-split!"

Carefully, Honey opened her mouth wide and held the cone in it. She carried the cone across the room without eating it.

Then she stood on her hind legs and tossed the cone up . . . up into the air.

*Poof!*

In one gulp, the ice cream—cone and all— disappeared into the dog's mouth.

The kids shouted with delight, "Do it again!"

Honey licked her chops and gave Ellen a kiss. Dunkum quickly made another small cone.

And Honey did the trick again.

Soon, it was time for the Cul-de-Sac Kids to go home. Dunkum followed his friends to the door.

"Thanks for the party," Carly said. She waved while her second ice-cream cone dripped off her hand. Vanilla drops dripped all the way down the sidewalk.

"Your party was fun, Dunkum," said Stacy. "Even the fried ants." She made a face and giggled with Abby.

"See you tomorrow." Dunkum waved to them.

That's when he saw something red flash in the bushes across the street!

White moonbeams cast their shadows on Blossom Hill Lane. Dunkum stared at the bushes.

Was someone in a red shirt hiding over there? Or were his eyes playing a trick on him?

# Four

**D**unkum rubbed his eyes, still watching.
*I saw something*, he thought. *I just know it!*

"It's bedtime," called his mother from the house.

Dunkum didn't go back inside. Instead, he ran across the street. He searched the bushes and found some old newspapers.

Then he saw an ID bracelet. Dunkum picked it up. The letters A. H. shone in the moonlight.

*A. H.? Must belong to Abby Hunter*, he thought.

Dunkum looked up the street. He could see Abby, Carly, and their adopted brothers walking with Stacy.

He shook his head. "There's no way Abby could have dropped this. Not way over here."

He stuffed the bracelet into his pocket and headed back across the street. Looking down, he saw vanilla ice-cream globs on the sidewalk. "What a mess," he whispered.

He remembered seeing Carly's ice-cream cone drip on the sidewalk as she left. He hurried inside to get some wet paper towels. He wanted to clean up the mess before his mother found it. And before any ants started showing up. "Mom hates ants," he muttered.

He left the front door open and dashed into the kitchen.

Ellen was still sitting at the table, humming softly. "I'm too tired to put Honey's harness back on," she said with a yawn.

Dunkum glanced at Honey. "Looks like she's zonked out," he said. "Here, I'll help you upstairs."

His mother was cleaning up the kitchen. "Okay if Honey sleeps here tonight, Mom?" Dunkum asked.

She looked at the sleeping dog under the table. "Honey looks comfortable right there."

Ellen stood up. "Sweet dreams, girl," she whispered to Honey. Then she blew a kiss.

Dunkum bent his right elbow and guided Ellen upstairs. "The party was fun," he said.

"I think Honey would have done that lickety-split trick at least two more times," Ellen said. "If we let her."

"Too much sugar might rot her teeth," Dunkum said. "Unless she brushes right away."

Ellen laughed.

"Well, good night," Dunkum said and headed to the kitchen.

Honey was still asleep under the table. Dunkum watched the steady rise and fall of her breathing. "Sleep tight, Honey," he said.

He hugged his parents good-night and went to his room. Putting on his pajamas, Dunkum thought of Adam Henny. Did he even own a pair of pj's?

Dunkum skipped saying his prayers tonight. He hopped into bed and snuggled down. Strings of moonbeams danced on the pillow as he fell asleep.

■ ■ ■

At midnight, Dunkum sat straight up in bed.

Something had popped into his memory. Something so important it woke him up!

"Oh," he groaned. "How could I forget?"

Grabbing his bathrobe, he darted through the hall and down the stairs. He flicked on the inside switch, flooding the front yard with light. Dunkum opened the front door and looked at the sidewalk.

*Phooey!*

The ants had already come. They were having an ice-cream party parade!

Dunkum tiptoed to the kitchen and yanked on the towel rack. The roll went flying. He crawled under the table and chased the roll of paper towels.

Right away, he noticed the empty spot under the table. Right where Honey had been sleeping.

"Honey?" he called softly, looking around the kitchen.

Dunkum placed the paper towel roll on the rack and rushed upstairs. He opened Ellen's door without making a sound. Peering into Ellen's room, he said, "Are you in there, Honey?"

Ellen made a squeaky little sound in her sleep.

He didn't want to awaken and worry her. So he closed the bedroom door and flew back downstairs.

He looked everywhere for Honey. In the living room, under the coffee table. He looked in the dining room, under the dinner table. He even looked in the garage.

"What's happened to Ellen's dog?" Dunkum whispered. He felt sick inside.

Honey was missing!

He sat on a kitchen chair and stared at the floor where Honey had slept. Where *was* she?

Ellen would need Honey first thing tomorrow. And Ellen's father was coming for her next week!

Dunkum had to find Honey.

Soon!

# Five

**D**unkum's heart pounded.

He grabbed a flashlight and headed to the dimly lit basement. Slowly, he shone his flashlight into the darkest corners. Light zigzagged across boxes of Christmas ornaments.

*Flash!* He shined the light on rows of canned goods. But Honey was nowhere in sight.

Dashing upstairs, Dunkum ran outside, past the party ants. He spotted something lying in the grass. At first, it looked like a fake red snake. He leaned down. "What's this?" he said softly.

It was a leather collar. Just like Honey's. Dunkum read the tags. It *was* Honey's collar!

His eyes caught sight of the swarm of ants. He'd forgotten again! But instead of going inside for paper towels, he marched to the outside faucet. He would hose down the ice-cream drippings, ants and all!

Just as Dunkum turned on the hose, a light flashed on above his head. He looked up to see his parents' bedroom filled with light.

*Rats!* he thought.

Turning off the hose, he ran toward the house.

But his father met him at the door. "What's going on, son? Why are you outside at midnight?"

Dunkum opened his mouth to speak.

"Don't you know what time it is?" His father tapped on his watch.

"It's late," Dunkum blurted, trying to explain. "I think Honey left the house." He held up her collar.

"You *think*?"

Dunkum's mother was coming down the stairs. He stood in the doorway, hoping to block her view of the ants.

Dad told Mom the bad news. "Dunkum says Honey's missing, dear."

"What?" Mom let out a little wail. "Are you sure? Have you searched the house and the yard?"

Dunkum nodded. "I've looked everywhere."

"Who was the last person to see Honey?" Dad asked.

Dunkum wasn't sure. "I think Ellen was the last person to see Honey." It sounded weird because Ellen couldn't see at all.

"You know, I had a strange feeling about Honey sleeping downstairs tonight." Dunkum's mom pushed the front door shut. "By the way, this door was standing wide open when I went to bed."

"It was?" Dunkum had forgotten that, too.

"Well, that's it, then," his father said. "Honey took off sometime after Ellen went to bed."

Dunkum felt horrible. Guide dogs were special. Lots of time went into training them. Lots of money, too. Besides that, Honey was part of the family.

A lump the size of a scoop of ice cream filled his throat.

Dunkum's mother pushed her bangs back. "Honey will probably come home when she's hungry."

"Hungry? That's it!" Dunkum shouted.

His parents watched in amazement as Dunkum led them out the front door. "I think I just remembered!" He pointed to the sidewalk.

His mom gasped. "Oh, look at those horrid ants!"

Dunkum tried to explain. "After the party, Carly's cone was dripping onto the sidewalk."

Suddenly, Dad seemed to understand. "And we all know how much Honey loves vanilla ice cream," he said. The lines in his forehead grew deeper.

"Honey must have followed the drips," Dunkum's mom said.

"So . . . she might be somewhere up the street," Dunkum said. "Maybe even at Abby's house." He started up the sidewalk.

"It's midnight," his mom called to him. "It's much too late to search now."

"That's right," Dad said. "Honey will be all right until morning."

But Dunkum was worried. Honey was trained to guide Ellen. Who knew what dangers were lurking in the midnight shadows?

Tears stung Dunkum's eyes. This was all his fault.

# Six

The next morning, Dunkum hurried downstairs.

Was Mom right? Had Honey come home for breakfast?

He searched the front yard, then the back. Honey was nowhere to be seen.

He ran through the neighborhood and asked the other Cul-de-Sac Kids if they'd seen Honey.

Nobody had.

"Let's trace the ice-cream trail," Abby suggested when she heard the whole story.

The kids agreed.

So, starting at Dunkum's house, they counted twenty ice-cream drops to Abby's house.

"Look, you can even see Honey's tongue marks," said Jason.

Eric looked closer. "Cannot."

"Gotcha!" hooted Jason.

Abby frowned, ignoring Jason. "Wouldn't Honey have eaten all the ice cream drips, though? Maybe she didn't follow them. What other clues do we have?" she asked Dunkum.

He showed them Honey's dog collar and the ID bracelet. "This is all I found last night."

Eric looked at the bracelet. He studied the initials. "A. H.? Maybe it belongs to Abby."

"It's not mine." Abby twisted her hair. "Think of all the kids we know with those initials."

"I'll make a list of people's names," Stacy offered.

"Good idea," Eric said.

The kids split up and hopped on their bikes. Up and down the street they rode, whistling and calling for Honey. They talked to each neighbor on Blossom Hill Lane. They even checked at the Humane Society, which picked up lost pets.

But no Honey.

At last, they followed Dunkum into his

house. Ellen was having breakfast. Her eyes were red from crying.

Dunkum raced into the kitchen. "We're going to find Honey for you," he said. "I promise."

"We'll do our detective best," Abby said and gave Ellen a hug.

"Let's put an ad in the paper," Dunkum said. "If someone sees Honey, we might get a phone call."

Abby suggested, "We could offer a reward."

"Hey, good thinking. That ought to help," Jason said. He held up the newspaper. "Look, here's someone offering twenty dollars for a brown beagle." The kids crowded around Jason.

Stacy pulled out a pencil and a pad. "If we each give some of our allowance, we'll have enough for a nice reward," she said.

"Don't count Ellen," Eric said. "It wouldn't be fair for her to put money into a reward."

"I think twenty bucks is too cheap," Dunkum said. "Let's go with five bucks each. That makes forty-five dollars."

"Not bad," said Dee Dee.

"I have more than that in my piggy bank," said Carly.

"Me too," said little Jimmy Hunter.

"It'll be worth it to have Honey back," Abby said. "Now, let's decide on our ad."

■■■

*LOST—*
*one golden Labrador guide dog.*
*Answers to Honey.*
*$45 reward.*
*Call 555-1028*
*or return to*
*233 Blossom Hill Lane.*

"I really hope this works," Ellen said. She wiped her eyes.

"We *all* do," said Dunkum.

# Seven

"Let's ride our bikes to the newspaper office," Dunkum said.

The Cul-de-Sac Kids called their good-byes to Ellen.

On the way, they saw a dogcatcher. Dunkum cringed. Honey had lost her collar last night. What if the dogcatcher found her? How would a beautiful, smart dog like Honey feel locked up with mangy mutts?

"Hey, mister!" Dunkum called. "Have you seen a golden Lab around the neighborhood?"

The other Cul-de-Sac Kids stopped pedaling.

Jimmy Hunter's eyes were as wide as

saucers. His older brother, Shawn, looked very worried. Carly and Dee Dee whispered to each other. Abby and Stacy were silent. Eric pulled his bike up next to Jason's.

The dogcatcher walked toward them, mopping his forehead. "Sorry, kids. No dogs like that around here."

"Thanks anyway," Dunkum said. He felt kind of sad. But glad, too, that Honey wasn't being treated as a stray.

The kids pushed on, past the corner store. When they came to the post office, Dunkum spotted Adam Henny. He was mailing a letter, wearing another one of his grubby outfits.

Dunkum sped up. He hoped Adam wouldn't see him. Because Adam Henny was the last person Dunkum wanted to talk to today.

"Hey, Dunkum! Wait up!" It was Adam shouting at him.

The other kids slowed down. Abby waved to Adam. So did Eric and Jason. Jimmy and Shawn rode their bikes over to Adam.

Dunkum gripped his handlebars and

watched his friends. He felt too tense. He did *not* want shabby Adam in their club!

"Where's everyone going?" Adam asked Abby.

Dunkum took a deep breath. He wanted to say, "Get lost."

But Abby said, "Ellen's dog is missing. We're putting an ad in the newspaper."

Adam looked surprised. "Honey's missing?"

"Uh, we better get going," Dunkum interrupted. He wanted to get away from Adam. Fast.

So he led the group, speeding off and leaving the boy behind once again.

"Dunkum, wait!" Adam called after them. But Dunkum would not look back.

■ ■ ■

At the newspaper office, Abby shoved her kickstand down. She glared at Dunkum. "What's your problem?" she asked. "You were rude to Adam. Why?"

"I don't want him in on our plans," Dunkum shouted back at her.

"What's the big deal? Nobody said it was a secret about Honey," Abby said. Her hands were on her hips. She seemed angry.

Eric stepped between them. "Don't yell at her, Dunkum. Abby didn't do anything wrong."

"Yeah, who cares if Adam knows?" Jason asked.

Dunkum was no dummy. Eric and Jason were sticking up for Abby. "Adam Henny isn't a Cul-de-Sac Kid. That's all," Dunkum muttered. "He's not in our club."

"Well, so what?" Stacy spoke up. "He's a human being, isn't he?"

The kids stared at her, surprised. Stacy hardly ever raised her voice.

"It doesn't matter if Adam is in our club or not," Abby shot back. "He can help us find Honey, can't he?"

Dunkum was afraid Abby might say that. No way should Adam get the reward money.

Eric shrugged his shoulders. "Adam's not so bad." He turned and followed Abby up the steps to the newspaper office.

The rest of the Cul-de-Sac Kids were close behind.

Dunkum stomped his foot. His summer was off to a rotten start. Thanks to a kid who needed a two-hour bath!

# Eight

When Dunkum arrived home, Ellen was reading her Braille joke book. "Listen to this," she said.

Dunkum sat down. He was glad Ellen couldn't see his face. He was also glad she couldn't see into his heart.

"Who was the world's first banker?" she asked.

"I don't know," said Dunkum, trying to sound interested.

"Pharaoh's daughter. She found a little prophet in the rushes to the banks." Ellen began to laugh. "Isn't that funny?"

"Yeah, real funny," Dunkum said, pouting.

"What's wrong with you?" Ellen asked, facing him.

"How can you read jokes and laugh when Honey's missing?"

"God will take care of Honey," she said.

Dunkum felt terrible. He was getting it from all sides. Excusing himself, he went to his room. Every few minutes, he could hear Ellen laughing out loud.

*The joke book must be very funny*, thought Dunkum.

He decided to sit in his room, all by himself.

■■■

An hour later, the doorbell rang. "I'll get it," Dunkum said. He rushed downstairs.

Eric Hagel stood on the porch.

"Hi, Eric. What's up?" Dunkum asked.

"Let's talk somewhere private," Eric said. His eyes blinked too fast.

"Come to my room," Dunkum said, leading the way.

"Where's that ID bracelet you showed us?" Eric asked.

Dunkum went to his dresser and picked up the bracelet. "What do you want with it?"

"I think I know who it belongs to," Eric

said. He took it from Dunkum. "I think A. H. stands for Adam Henny."

Dunkum gasped. "Of course!" Why hadn't he thought of that?

"But . . . we don't know for sure," Eric added.

"It makes sense, though, doesn't it?" Dunkum said.

"Only if Adam dropped it in the bushes last night," Eric said.

"Adam must have been spying on our party," Dunkum decided.

"That's strange." Eric sat on Dunkum's bed. "Do you think this is a dognapping case?" he asked.

"Beats me," Dunkum said. "Let's have a club meeting. We'll see what the rest of the Cul-de-Sac Kids think."

"Ellen should come, too," Eric said.

"You're right. She has sort of a sixth sense," Dunkum said.

They hurried downstairs to get Ellen.

■ ■ ■

The club meeting was in Abby's backyard. She called the meeting to order. Then she said, "Any new business?"

Dunkum held up the ID bracelet. "Eric and I have a theory. We think this clue might lead us to Honey."

Abby and Stacy sat in the grass, twirling their hair.

Carly and Dee Dee were all ears. "What's a theory?" asked Dee Dee.

"It's like a guess," Dunkum explained.

"I don't want to guess about Honey," Jimmy said.

Shawn shook his head. He was worried about Honey, too.

Eric was grinning. "Dunkum and I believe that this ID bracelet belongs to Adam Henny."

Abby's mouth flew open. "Why do you think that?"

"For one thing, we know only two kids with the initials A.H.," Dunkum said. He glanced at Abby.

Ellen asked to hold the ID bracelet. She had a strange look on her face as she touched it.

"If this *does* belong to Adam," Dunkum said, "I think we're looking at a dognapping."

"What?" Abby and Ellen said together.

"It could be a case for the police," Dunkum said. Talking about the police made him feel much better.

If Adam Henny was to blame, maybe *then* he'd leave them alone.

# Nine

The next day, Dunkum talked to Abby after Sunday school. "I'm sorry about yesterday," he said.

"You were upset. So was I." She paused for a moment. "You know what?"

"What?" asked Dunkum.

"I'm sorry, too," she said.

Dunkum waited in line at the water fountain. "Did you see our ad in the morning paper?" he asked.

Abby smiled, her eyes shining. "It looked terrific. But something's strange. There were sixteen pets reported missing over the weekend."

"Wow, that's a lot," Dunkum said.

"I think something's going on," she said.

"What do you mean?" Dunkum asked.

"I did some checking," Abby told him. "I called six of the people who placed ads for lost pets."

"You did?" Dunkum was all ears. "What did they say?"

"It seems that a bald man in a black Jeep has been returning lost pets," said Abby. "Sounds a lot like the guy we saw with Mister Whiskers. And, get this. Each owner had offered a reward."

Dunkum whistled. "What a nice guy."

"Unless he's stealing them first and giving them back for money," Abby said.

"Hey, what a rotten thing to do!" Dunkum said.

"If we could just find that man, maybe we'd find Honey," Abby said.

Dunkum was silent, thinking.

"Wait a minute!" Abby's eyes danced. "If Adam *was* spying in the bushes, maybe he saw something that night."

"Like what?" Dunkum asked.

"Maybe he saw the man driving his Jeep

around Blossom Hill Lane, waiting to steal Honey!"

"I think you might be on to something," said Dunkum.

He hoped so.

■■■

The Cul-de-Sac Kids had another meeting. This time, near a rundown cottage. Shutters were drooping off their hinges. Paint was peeling off the door. Adam Henny's house was a mess.

"Let's find out what Adam knows," Dunkum told the Cul-de-Sac Kids. He led his fellow detectives across the street.

Abby carried the ID bracelet. Stacy held Honey's leather collar. The kids lined up on Adam's front steps.

Dunkum poked the doorbell. He hoped they were doing the right thing.

The screen door opened. A woman with white hair peeked through. "May I help you?"

*Gulp!* Dunkum didn't know what to say. Was this the right house?

Abby stepped up to the door. "Is Adam home?"

The woman smiled. "Oh, he's down the street."

Abby held up the ID bracelet. "Does this belong to Adam?"

The woman nodded. "He's been looking everywhere for it."

Eric spoke up. "Tell him Dunkum Mifflin found it Friday night—in the bushes on our street."

The woman raised her eyebrows. "Friday night, you say?"

"That's right," Dunkum replied. *She must be Adam's grandma*, he thought.

"Well, now, let me think." The woman frowned for a moment. "Adam said he went to a party after the school play. A special party."

"Special?" Abby asked. She looked at Dunkum and the others. There was a question in her eyes.

"Oh yes, and Adam was so pleased," the woman said. "He told me his friends had the party just for him." The wrinkled corners of her mouth curved up. "Is it possible that you are those friends?"

"Uh, no, not really," Dunkum said quickly.

The woman's smile faded. She looked down at the ID bracelet in her hand. "Thanks for returning this. I'll see that Adam gets it."

"Where *is* Adam exactly?" Dunkum asked.

"Just two streets down," she said. "Maybe you can catch him. He's playing detective today, his favorite game."

The kids said good-bye and walked down the steps.

"Sounds like Adam's super lonely," Abby said.

"He'd have to be to make up a story like that," Stacy whispered.

Dunkum heard what Abby and Stacy said. *Having pretend friends can't be any fun*, he thought.

"Any kid who lies about going to a party must be desperate!" Abby said.

"No kidding," Eric said.

Shawn and Jimmy were nodding their heads.

Carly and Dee Dee looked very sad.

Jason did not dance or jive. He stood still for the first time in a long time.

Suddenly, Dunkum wished he could change things for Adam. And he knew just what he must do!

# Ten

The Cul-de-Sac Kids ran down two streets and turned the corner. "Look for Adam's bike," Dunkum said. "It's a faded green one with lots of rust."

They didn't have to look too long. The old bike was propped up against a police car. Three houses down.

Abby gasped. "What are the police doing here?"

"Let's find out." Dunkum led the way to the house.

Adam was sitting on the front step. "Hi, Dunkum. What are *you* doing here?" he asked.

"Your grandmother sent us," Dunkum said.

Adam's eyes widened. "She did?"

"She said you were playing detective," Jason said.

Adam's face lit up as two policemen brought a balding man outside. The man was handcuffed.

"Wow! My theory was right," Abby said.

The policemen led the man to the patrol car. They put him in the backseat and zoomed off.

Dunkum stared at Adam. He hardly noticed the boy's crummy old clothes. "Looks like you're an excellent detective."

Adam beamed a smile. "Thanks." He told them how he'd tracked down the balding guy. "It started Friday night. I was spying on your party. After everyone left, Honey wandered outside. The front door was wide open."

"My fault," Dunkum muttered.

"I sat on the curb just petting her," Adam said.

"And then what happened?" Dunkum asked.

Adam sighed. "I saw a black Jeep at the end of the street. It was real late, so I said good-bye to Honey and went home. I didn't even suspect the balding guy stole Honey. Not till yesterday."

Abby asked, "What made you curious about him?"

"You told me about your ad, remember?" Adam replied.

Dunkum felt a lump in his throat. Things were finally starting to make sense.

"How'd you ever find this house?" Eric asked.

"I saw the guy and his Jeep in the driveway. I called 9-1-1 and told the police what I'd seen after the party."

"So . . . where's Honey now?" Dunkum asked.

"In the backyard, waiting to go home." Adam got up and went around the side of the house. He returned with Honey.

The Cul-de-Sac Kids cheered and rushed to her. Honey's gentle eyes seemed to say, *I'm glad you found me.*

Dunkum thanked Adam for his detective work. "Ellen always believed Honey would be safe," he said. "She missed her dog, but she never worried."

"I should have told you right away what I

saw," Adam admitted. "Please tell Ellen I'm sorry I waited."

"Why don't you tell her yourself?" Dunkum said.

"Really?" Adam's face burst into a giant grin. "Do you mean it?"

"Lickety-split!" Dunkum said to Honey. And she ran between him and Adam.

Abby and the others dashed close behind. They arrived at Dunkum's house, out of breath.

Dunkum told Adam about Honey's ice-cream trick.

Adam's eyes lit up. "Honey does tricks?"

Dunkum nodded and called to Ellen. "Guess who's hungry for a vanilla cone!"

Ellen squealed with delight from her room. "Oh, come here, girl!"

Honey raced upstairs, tail wagging.

"Don't forget about the reward money," Abby said.

But Adam shook his head. "I didn't do this for the money." He looked straight at Dunkum. "But I *do* want something."

Dunkum was sure what Adam wanted.

The boy who needed new clothes also needed a friend.

Hurrying inside to the kitchen, Dunkum opened the freezer. He reached for a box of ice cream. "It's time to throw a party for a fellow detective." He smiled at Adam Henny.

And Adam smiled back.

## About the Author

Beverly Lewis thinks all the Cul-de-Sac Kids are super fun. She clearly remembers growing up on Ruby Street in her Pennsylvania hometown. She and her younger sister, Barbara, played with the same group of friends year after year. Some of those childhood friends appear in her Cul-de-Sac Kids series—disguised, of course!

Now Beverly lives with her husband, David, in Colorado, where she enjoys writing books for all ages. Beverly loves to tell stories, but because the Cul-de-Sac Kids series is for children, it will always have a special place in her heart.

Learn more about Beverly and her books at www.BeverlyLewis.com.